"We're

"Gella Icor?" Conek's voice was hoarse with disbelief. "There's got to be some mistake."

"Danzic Icor committed the crime," the minister said, as if that explained the matter.

"I can't believe that either. Besides, Icor's dead—dead for almost two years."

"So his daughter will pay his penalty for him."

Conek wondered if he was going space happy. "But she's not guilty!"

"Of course she is," the minister softly insisted. "The stain of his guilt is on all those who carry his blood. It is our way, what our religion teaches us."

Conek found the minister's friendly calm more threatening than if he had ranted and screamed.

"And the cynbeth?"

"The creature will be put to death also."

"It's an infant!" Conek protested. "It has nothing to do with this!" Conek had faced Vladmn Patrols, assassins, and warships—but religious insanity was something else again.

"It came with her," the minister smiled, "and she must pay for her father's crime . . ."

STARFIRE DOWN

Also by Lee McKeone

GHOSTER
BACKBLAST

ATTENTION: SCHOOLS AND CORPORATIONS

WARNER books are available at quantity discounts with bulk purchase for educational, business, or sales promotional use. For information, please write to: SPECIAL SALES DEPARTMENT, WARNER BOOKS, 666 FIFTH AVENUE, NEW YORK, N.Y. 10103.

**ARE THERE WARNER BOOKS
YOU WANT BUT CANNOT FIND IN YOUR LOCAL STORES?**

You can get any WARNER BOOKS title in print. Simply send title and retail price, plus 50¢ per order and 50¢ per copy to cover mailing and handling costs for each book desired. New York State and California residents add applicable sales tax. Enclose check or money order only, no cash please, to: WARNER BOOKS, P.O. BOX 690, NEW YORK, N.Y. 10019.

STARFIRE DOWN

LEE McKEONE

WARNER BOOKS

A Time Warner Company

WARNER BOOKS EDITION

Copyright © 1991 by Dixie Lee McKeone
All rights reserved.

Questar® is a registered trademark of Warner Books, Inc.

Cover illustration by James Warhola
Cover design by Don Puckey

Warner Books, Inc.
666 Fifth Avenue
New York, NY 10103

W A Time Warner Company

Printed in the United States of America

First Printing: May, 1991

10 9 8 7 6 5 4 3 2 1

STARFIRE DOWN

CHAPTER 1

The gray of time-comp dissolved into the blackness of space, lit by pinpoints of distant stars. Yellow, white, orange, red; the green came in a streak of color passing harmlessly a good distance away.

"Someone's shooting at somebody!"

Gella Icor recognized that streak as the fire pattern of an old-style ship's blaster. Though she was only eighteen years old, she had seen enough space battles to react with speed and precision.

"It's not good manners to interrupt a war," she said and hit a button on the control panel. Beneath it were three letters: N O W.

To most private citizens of the tri-galactic Vladmn Territory the letters would appear to be an acronym for some incredibly complicated piece of equipment. Those were the honest plodders whose main fear in life was having the trash disintegrator malfunction, or missing the newest holo film when it was broadcast on vidcom.

The equipment activated by that button was complicated, an emergency program, set with alternate coordinates for making a quick getaway. To Gella Icor, and to her father who had installed the system, the three letters formed the word "NOW," as in *move your tail or get it shot off*.

As *Starfire* grayed into time-comp again, the girl settled back in the pilot's seat and adjusted the two hairbands that confined her hair. If the ship's gravity failed, she could be smothered by the loose mass of long auburn waves and curls that framed a heart-shaped face.

She ran a check on *Starfire*'s weapons and sat back, turning her head to gaze across the cockpit.

High on the back of the copilot's seat, a pocket of hastily rigged webbing held a small red-gold reptile. He was a cynbeth and closely resembled a dragon from the mythical days of old Earth. At four months old, he was still considered an infant of his species; his body was shorter than her hand.

"One of the first lessons you have to learn is don't get in someone else's fight," she told the little creature. "One side or the other will get upset."

"Chirk!" The little reptile lowered himself in the webbing pouch until only his head showed over his protection. He gave a short hiss in the direction of the view screen.

Gella wondered if little Red, as she'd named him, could understand her. Cynbeth males were not only sentient, but highly intelligent. Most needed translators to understand or communicate. But most were raised on their home planet, and never saw another sentient species until they were adults. Red had been hatched aboard Conek Hayden's freighter, *Destria*, and had spent a good part of his short life in the company of humans.

He apparently liked humans, so much so that he had hidden himself in Gella's gear. She had been a galaxy away when she discovered her unexpected passenger.

As if she didn't have problems enough, with a heavy schedule, one sluggish thruster, and a comm-unit that worked only intermittently, she was worried over what Sis-Silsis's reaction would be to the loss of one of his youngsters. The little ex-smuggler had three hundred and twenty-six others, but he kept a parental eye on each one. A planetary plague had nearly destroyed their species, and few of the cynbeth males who survived were capable of producing progeny. Every slither, as they called their young, was precious.

Starfire wasn't in the gray of time-comp long. Gella's emergency coordinates brought them back into normal space in a matter of minutes, halfway across the solar system from her original position. She came out with every sensor active, but she saw no sign of a space battle.

"Probably just some patrol chasing a pirate." She doubted they would be after any of her old buddies in the smuggling community. She had never heard of a profitable illegal product in this section of Alpha Galaxy.

She made her computations for landing on Neocar, the small, low-gravity, fourth planet in the Halmarin system. She eased her way around a dense asteroid belt and checked the region again before streaking for the small agricultural world.

"After this, we have one more delivery," she told Red as the ship settled beside a large farming complex at the top of a small hill. She taxied the ship until it was close to a series of large structures that appeared to be warehouses.

"We'll get rid of this what's-it stuff and be on our way."

"Chirk?"

"I don't know, some sort of chemical fertilizer that force-grows fruit." She gave an automatic reply to what might have been the slither's question. She checked the manifest and wondered if help would come from any of the buildings. The place looked to be deserted. Anyone within kilometers would have heard the ship land. She wondered if she would have to off-load by herself, and what to do if there was no one to sign for the delivery.

Then, looking out over the kilometers of fields, she saw a roil of dust that hid an approaching vehicle.

"Here comes the cavalry," she said, relaxing and unfastening her safety harness. Help was still kilometers away. She thought she might have time to grab a snack before unloading.

She heard a drone of a ship overhead. A check of the identification sensor showed the new arrival to be a Kalviton freighter, a slow drone of an inter-system ship that had been modified for speed and additional range. The incoming vessel had never been an efficient cargo carrier, and most of its space had been given over to four additional thrusters. She mentally calculated the remaining cargo space aboard the ship and thought it might hold a case of vita fluid and three small holo cubes.

Over her head the communications speaker was chattering and hissing, but she couldn't make out a word. Experience of the trouble had already taught her she could not transmit while it was malfunctioning.

As the ship dropped lower she could see it through the view screen. No registration markings. She didn't like that.

"Now what are we into?" she asked, and opened a small storage compartment on her right. She pulled out a belt attached to a blaster holster. Unfastening her safety straps, she belted on the weapon carrier, pulled the blaster from its case, and checked the charge.

Red watched her with bright eyes, gave another hiss and a couple of barks.

"It can't be anything much," she said as she cleared *Starfire*'s weaponry in case she had to fight her way out. "If they belong here, they'll have a copy of our manifest. If they're pirates, they don't want our load. You stay where you are."

When the modified freighter cut its thrusters, the ramp lowered and she watched as four humanoids came marching down the ramp and started toward her ship. She gave a sigh of relief. They were dressed alike in some sort of full dress uniforms, glittering with gold braid. Blue jackets, red pants, yellow stripes, green hats, they hadn't missed a chance for color. The leader wore a vile purple sash over his left shoulder, most of which was hidden under the sparkling medals pinned to the shiny cloth.

"The local law and order," she said, closing down the ship's weapons system and removing her blaster belt. Before the uniformed quartet reached *Starfire*, Gella had the ramp down and was waiting for them. Red had climbed out of his safety harness and was crouched by her feet.

"No hissing or barking," she told him. "We're good guys now, remember?"

She watched them approach and decided they were Halmarins. Though this was her first time in their area—they didn't travel out of their own solar system—she recognized them from the pictures she had seen. They were humanoid, the tallest stood just over a meter in height. Something in their genes must have remembered a time when they were larger, because their skin was loose and hung in folds as if waiting for them to continue growing and fill it.

When they saw her standing at the top of the ramp they paused, conferred together, and one pulled his weapon. The leader motioned him to put it away and they came forward again, the one with the sash in front, and the other three in a stiff, straight line behind him.

"Did you try to contact me?" Gella called out. "I'm having trouble with my communications system. Would you have anyone on board that could take a look at it?"

State a legitimate problem if she had one and ask for help was a rule her father had taught her. If the Halmarins didn't believe her, they could see for themselves that she couldn't reply. Winning a little sympathy couldn't hurt.

The leader stopped at the foot of the ramp. He ignored her questions and explanation.

"I am Colonel Hubrin of the Benevolent Aid and Peace Assistance Authority," he said and paused.

"And blessed be all his line," the three behind him spoke in a unified drone.

Yeah, they were the local law enforcement, Gella thought, not liking the name they gave it. The more loudly a title shouted sweetness and light, the more it could cloak. This group was protesting its innocence the first time it announced itself. Not a good sign.

"We fired a shot across your path, ordering you to halt when you entered our system."

"Sorry, I didn't understand," Gella said, thinking they certainly had a way of catching a person's attention. "I'm just hauling freight and it never occurred to me that I could be the target. As I said before, my communications are out."

"Why are you here?" Colonel Hubrin demanded.

"I'm scheduled to deliver a load of"—what was the name

of the what's-it stuff? She pulled out her small record computer and activated it—"Olvacill to this agricultural base. You're welcome to inspect the cargo and look over the manifest."

"I've no interest in olvacill," the colonel said. "Who are you delivering it to?"

"A Car-Marlin." She held out the record keeper, willing to let the colonel take a look. Play it innocent all the way. Pretty good game, since this time it was for real.

"And blessed be all his line," the three men behind the colonel intoned as she gave the name of the client.

The litany put Gella off. She forgot what she meant to say next, and decided she had better identify herself.

"I fly for Hayden Haulers, run by Conek Hayden. His—"

"And blessed be all his line," came the chant, interrupting her again. She took a deep breath, attempting to get her mind back on course.

"We're a registered company, licensed to carry cargo anywhere in the three galaxies of Vladmn," she said, hurrying to finish. "I'm a limited permit pilot, Gella Icor—" She paused but this time the chant did not come. What was this? Didn't her relatives deserve a litany? So Icor had been a smuggler; they weren't all that bad.

"This ship is registered to Dansiz Icor," Hubrin snapped. "Why did he not come out to meet us? He was brave enough on Halmarin-II when he killed ten of our people and blew up their ship."

"What?" Gella stared at the colonel, stunned by his accusation. "Icor? There has to be some mistake! My father never killed anyone."

"He is a smuggler, an outlaw—" the colonel started his accusations, but Gella cut him off.

"Yes, he *was* a contrabandist, but—" How had Conek put it not long after Icor's death? He had his limits. Vladmn had considered him small-time, an irritant, one they'd like to catch, but not important nor dangerous enough to be high on the list of priorities.

"I'll admit he was a smuggler, but never a killer," she protested.

Hearing her anger and the force of her voice, Red, who had been crouching at her feet, gave a hiss and took several steps forward, spreading his wings.

Seeing the Halmarins eyeing the little cynbeth and fingering their side arms, Gella reached down and picked up the slither, stroking his back to calm him.

"*Was?*" the colonel snapped. "Has he gone to his ancestors unpunished?"

"Unpunished for what?" Gella demanded. "He didn't harm any of your people."

"He is dead?" Hubrin demanded again.

"He was killed almost two years ago," she said, reliving part of her grief in the admission.

"You will come with us," the colonel ordered. He pulled his blaster. His companions did the same.

CHAPTER 2

"Three of my new plants are blooming," Ulcher said. The holo image of the amphibian was hazy, but clear enough to show his gills were fluttering as if he were submerged, a certain indication that he was under stress. Scared silly was a better description.

Lagon Fellerd crouched on eight of his ten stalk legs, looking as if he were ready to spring at the oversize holo on his desk. The threat of the cleosar's stance usually intimidated its intended victim, even through the holo. After the momentary delay of the hyperspace transmission, the helovan's image on the desktop flinched, but appeared to be too concerned with his message to feel himself further endangered.

The casual chitchat sounded as if the cleosar and the helovan were old friends, but nearly every phrase held its own coded meaning. The blooming of three plants meant a vital shipment had not arrived.

"You always were clever with your plants," Fellerd answered. *What happened*? was what he actually said.

"I believe it was the new composite plant food I've been feeding them."

Fellerd's two front legs folded in on themselves as he dug his agile claws into the pads attached to the sides of his desk. By ripping at the tough, self-mending archon surface he worked off his growing frustration as he mentally sorted through his list of words, translated meanings and swore to himself. The shipment had been captured. The pilot had been arrested. The word "plant" indicated it had been local authorities, not the Vladmn Patrol, which would have called for the use of "fertilization." New composite—that wasn't a part of the code. Something had happened they had not prepared for.

He'd slaughter that Olynthr councilor for talking him into using Hayden Haulers. He should have followed his first inclination and stayed away from a company that had an ex-smuggler for an owner.

That was what came of playing political games, only he needed Olynthr to complete the plan for Beta Galaxy. He needed the councilor to get a hold on the planet. The councilor needed to catch the attention of the quinta. Norden would be pleased if he gave Hayden Haulers a chance. Everyone got what they wanted, only Fellerd's shipment to Vilarona had not arrived.

What had happened to it? He stared at the holo in frustration, knowing he could not ask. Had the authorities been on the watch for his shipment? They were always on watch, but had they caught on to his methods? What had they done with it?

He had covered his tracks with extreme care. They should not be able to trace it back to him. Was there some way to trace it back to Ulcher? Was that why he looked so scared?

"I wonder if I should try raising Charchich lowblossoms," Fellerd asked as if their conversation were still simply horticultural.

"I've never had any luck with them," Ulcher replied. His gills fluttered more strongly. "Very few people know anything about them."

Stars and quasars, they—whoever they were who had taken

the pilot and the ship—didn't know what they had. Ulcher had not been able to find the vessel.

No wonder he was terrified.

Fellerd could relax. No one was going to trace the shipment back to him. If Ulcher was telling the truth, before long there would be no shipment to investigate. There'd be no ship that brought it in. And if he was in the general vicinity, there would be no Ulcher to panic.

"What do you think about that new species they are trying over on the NearArm in Alpha?" he asked thoughtfully. "I've been wanting to get out there and take a look. I've been hearing they're getting good results on Tri-four in the Jolwain system. Haven't had time."

"I'd consider it," Ulcher said doubtfully, as if he weren't sure of Fellerd's meaning.

"If *you* find the opportunity to get into that region, you might take a look and let me know what you think," Fellerd suggested. When the transmission had reached Vilarona and returned, the helovan's gills had calmed. The cleosar had not realized the thick-bodied aquatic had been trembling, but he noticed the stillness.

Yes, he was right. Ulcher was one of the few in his network who knew what was in those shipments. He was right to get them out before they panicked.

He closed off the transmission and paced his office, his three-fingered clawed feet clicking on the gleaming floor. Outside, the bright sunlight that flooded the careful landscaping of the business complex glittered down at him from the top of the cavern that made up the city of Agnar-West. If the designers of the underground city felt the need for weather conditions to make the citizens feel more comfortable, why couldn't they have cloudy weather once in a while? He turned back to the electronic console behind his desk and partially fogged the transparencies. He could think better if he didn't have to squint.

What had happened? How could it have happened?

His shipments had to go through on time, or the plans were going to crumble around his feet.

Disintegrate was a better word, not only for the plans, but for his customers if those shipments didn't get through.

And why had that pilot been arrested?

Ulcher could stop worrying. He might be afraid of bringing bad news to a cleosar, but he didn't have Fellerd's trouble.

At least Ulcher didn't have to report to someone who might eat him.

CHAPTER 3

A human female three tables away was eyeing Conek Hayden. She appeared tallish, but he wasn't sure since she was sitting down. Her skin was a golden tan, her hair a honey blond. If both were natural she could be from his home planet of Colsar.

She sat with another female, but she kept throwing glances in his direction.

Conek resisted the urge to sit up straighter. He was on the tall side, his honey-blond hair was natural and decently cut and generally went the way it wanted. Women did notice him from time to time, often enough so he wasn't startled by it, but he wasn't jaded by it either.

He was flattered and irritated; flattered because she was exactly the type of woman he had been thinking of when he decided to give up wrong-side running and turn legal. Her type didn't haunt smuggler worlds. He was irritated because he had to forget her and give his attention to his guest who was a potential client of that legal business.

He leaned back in the plush grav-chair, took a swallow of his drink, and glanced out of the transparency. From the height of forty stories above the street, he and his guest had an excellent view of the main cavern of Agnar-Alpha, the capital city of the tri-galactic Vladmn Territory.

Non-spacers, or moles as the spacers called the Agnar-Alphans, seemed to get a thrill out of the location. Conek's bribe to the seater of AllWorlds restaurant had bought him a table by the window.

As an inter-galactic freighter pilot, he was used to seeing real skies and stars. The restaurant on the top floor of the tall office building brought him too close to the stone ceiling of that mammoth cave. From the street it resembled a blue sky with clouds, but from the window the clouds were showing the dirt and dust of the city below; he could see the painted wires that gave power to the night stars.

But then that was Agnar-Alpha. He had planned, worked, and risked his life to get there. He should be enjoying it.

He turned his attention back to his guest, a squat, square humanoid whose small pig eyes stared at his host from behind a hairy face. Conek nodded as Tipple Chank explained how he operated his import company. He went into detail about the importance of having his deliveries made on time and how the rarities he sold were guaranteed to arrive undamaged. Every word he spoke was carefully chosen to let Conek know Chank's considerable reputation rode on honest business ethics.

His spiel would have seemed sincere if Conek had not known Chank when he was making his pile by dealing in contraband. They were playing a game. By unadmitted consent, their memories were shortened to forget those days.

Like most ex-wrong-side runners, Chank had made respectability his god when he turned honest.

But Chank was adding an extra dimension to the charade. By his careful choice of words Conek knew he carried a miniature long-playing recorder in the pocket of his tunic. The knowledge gave Conek a weapon of his own.

"So, you're saying I can trust your agents to make sure there's no contraband hidden in the shipments?"

Chank shifted in his chair. If he ever wanted to use the tapes to prove his innocence, he would also expose his answer to that question. His hesitation told Conek the recording was being made on the new sealed crystal system that once used could not be changed. It was the only vocal record accepted by the courts.

"I have made every effort to employ agents with impeccable reputations," Chank said slowly, carefully skirting a direct answer. His small, restless eyes watched Conek, knew he had not given a satisfactory answer, and looked away as if he could find one among the tables of the restaurant. Then he stiffened, his attention caught by someone crossing the room. His expression turned wary and he sat frozen like a wild creature willing himself to invisibility.

Conek turned his head to follow the humanoid's gaze and swore to himself. The man crossing the room was small, slightly built, and had all the visible masculine traits of a Colsarian cream dessert. His curling hair, pink and white complexion, and large blue eyes gave him the look of a pretty child.

Conek immediately recognized Major Andro Avvin, chief of the local spaceport authority. He was a small man outweighed by his courage. Even when Conek had still been a smuggler, he and Andro had cooperated to prevent the Osalts, Vladmn's enemy, from getting a powerful alien weapon. Later, during the recent rebellion, the major had been the military strategist that had turned the tide against the Amal. Future historians would probably discount the major's victory over two comet cruisers by making himself the sole target for their combined guns. His kind of desperate bravery in a crisis was seldom believed.

Behind Andro's pretty face and affected mannerisms was one of the finest minds in the tri-galactic Vladmn Territory. Conek had a great respect for the major, but at the moment he was the least welcome person in the room. All it would take to scare away Conek's potential client was for Andro to come mincing up. Just by his presence he would remind Conek's prospective client that Hayden Tri-Galactic Haulers was run by an ex-contrabandist.

But Andro wasn't mincing. He had left the affected facade behind. His expression said trouble. He had reached the table before he even noticed Chank. He blinked in confusion and went into one of his acts, giving them both a sweet smile.

"My dear, I have not lost my mind, have I?" he said to Conek. "Our engagement for lunch was not for today after all?"

"For later this week, I think," Conek replied, wondering what the major was up to. They traveled in different social circles.

"Then that's all right," Andro said with feigned relief. "When I saw you sitting here, I thought I had forgotten something—I have—" The major's large blue eyes opened as he affected a little lost-boy look. "Do *you* know who I was to meet today?"

"Probably your aunt," Conek said, watching Andro's speaking eyes, but unable to read the message. He could understand just enough to know that Andro had come in search of him, and brought trouble, not the kind he could discuss in front of Chank.

"You may be right. If she comes looking for me, I'll be in the waterfall room." Andro gave them another smile and wandered away.

Chank was unable to hide his relief or his curiosity.

"You're a friend of Major Avvin's?"

"You might say so." Conek was doing his relationship with the head of Agnar-Alpha's port authority an injustice. Theirs was a comradeship so strong each would unhesitatingly put their lives and reputations in the hands of the other. Socially they weren't friends, but they were too close in times of trouble for Conek to explain to his pig-eyed prospective client.

"You must be if you know his aunt," the humanoid said, and Conek remembered Chank came from a culture where any knowledge of another member's life or family was considered to make them vulnerable.

"It's hard not to know Quinta Norden," Conek said, watching Chank's swine-sized eyes widen. He was just the type to be impressed with name dropping.

"She and I have had our differences, but we're on reasonable terms now." He added the last to make sure the importer understood he wasn't in any trouble with any part of the government.

He'd read Tipple Chank correctly. The hairy humanoid immediately forgot Conek's past. He was already envisioning the reaction of his friends when he casually dropped the information that he was a friend of a friend of Quinta Norden's, and had met her nephew. In ten minutes a signed contract for two years of exclusive shipping was in Conek's hand, and he was saying good-bye to the squat little Cerlovian as they parted after lunch.

The blond woman had finished her lunch and left.

Conek left Chank at the gravator and went immediately to the waterfall room where pseudo-nooks gave small tables an illusion of privacy and where some of the most expensive drinks in the galaxy were served.

He found Andro sitting by himself, a cup of feine on the table.

"Sorry if I interrupted," Andro said as Conek took a seat across the table from him. He didn't look apologetic. He was preoccupied.

"I got the contract," Conek replied. "But you didn't show up to check on the financial success of Hayden Hauling."

Andro stared down at the cup in front of him, fingered the holder, and shifted his seat. "Is Gella Icor still flying for you?"

"You know she is," Conek said. "What's up?"

"Remember Lieutenant Pulkin?" At the shake of Conek's head the major went on. "He was one of my squadron in the rebellion. He remembers Gella and that old CD. He's patrolling over in Alpha's FarArm now."

Conek's lips tightened. Gella was making deliveries in that area. He couldn't remember what or just where, but he had a general idea of where all his people were working.

"What was her cargo?" Andro asked.

"Mostly agricultural supplies. Nothing to interest your people."

Andro wasn't convinced. "You're sure? Not that I think you'd risk Icor's daughter—"

"I wouldn't risk her *or* me. The Warehouses and *Windsong* make legitimate hauling too profitable."

He didn't try to fool himself or Andro. He had never had an objection to making a living by evading the customs charges on the many worlds in Vladmn Territory. His father had been a smuggler and for years Conek had followed in the same profession. But the life was limiting. Once he had enough ships and the financial buffer to try for the lucrative legal contracts, he had made the switch. His four huge Osalt freighters could haul three times what a regular Vladmn ship could carry, which had earned them the nickname Flying Warehouses. With *Windsong*, the far larger Skooler ship added to the fleet, he could make more money legally. It was also safer. He could count on being in business longer. In addition to his five ships, he had hired Gella with her own ship and Ister the Orelian with his Lapper, both good pilots with dependable vessels. He didn't need or want to go back to wrong-side running.

"Check, see what she was carrying," Andro urged.

Conek's irritation rose and faded. The major's facade could fool a lot of people, but not Conek. They had been through too much together. Andro wasn't on the trail of suspect cargo, that wasn't his field.

Hayden Tri-Galactic Haulers was not large enough to have an established office. Conek carried a miniaturized file in his personal computer. He pulled out the flat instrument, unfolded it, and punched in the access code. A string of products and destinations tripped across the screen in flickering green letters.

"Like I said, mostly stuff to do with agriculture," he muttered as he read the list. "She's delivered Erpidian breather masks for the mills on Jardos, replacement sensors for the mechanical harvesters on Gilarthy—" He read off the products and destinations in green. From Alpha FarArm, Gella had sent the "completed" code for those he had mentioned. The rest were in yellow, still to be delivered. He frowned. She was a full day off schedule.

"She's on her way to Neocar to deliver a shipment of

olvacill—some sort of soil enricher. Then she's for Vilarona with precidine. They mix it with a local paint to protect the mechanical agri-units. Like I said, nothing to interest anyone but the shippers."

He folded the file computer with a snap and stared at the major.

"So what's the trouble?"

"She landed on Neocar. When *Starfire* rose, she wasn't flying it."

"What?"

"Lieutenant Pulkin contacted the ship—"

"Why was he after her?"

Andro grinned. "Nothing official, she's a pretty girl." His smile faded. "*Starfire* was being taken off Neocar by the Halmarin planetary patrol. She's been taken into custody. The pilot of the CD couldn't or wouldn't tell Pulkin why."

"Must be a mistake," Conek said, hoping he was right but half sure he wasn't. He came equipped with some little emotional critter that walked up and down his backbone when trouble was in the making, and the creature was stomping its way up between his shoulder blades.

"I've seen to it she stayed strictly white hat," Conek said, as if reinforcing the fact that Agnar-Alpha would help Gella on Halmarin-IV. "They've probably banned some chemical and haven't notified the other worlds or the shippers. We'll end up paying a fine. Nothing in her cargo was illegal on Halmarin—according to my records."

"Then we'd better straighten it out and fast," Andro said. "She can't stay there long."

"No, I need her ship; we've got contracts to fill."

"We have to get her out for another reason," Andro said, leaning forward. "What do you know about Halmarin-IV?"

"What's to know? It's a humanoid planet." No one could keep up with all the details of the hundreds of thousands of settled worlds, and more were being colonized all the time.

"It was settled five hundred years ago," Andro explained. "Its prospects looked good for a few years—"

"Do we need to go through this?" Conek complained. He

wanted to get to his ship and on the way to Halmarin-IV. He could pick up the statistics on the way.

"Yes, we do," Andro insisted. "About fifty years after they settled the planet they did some heavy blasting to open up a mine. They released pockets of clin-gas. At first there wasn't enough to do much damage, but now the atmosphere is saturated with it. The Halmarins developed an immunity to it, but for us it's trouble."

"How much?"

"Breathed for too long, it destroys the chemical balance in humans. I don't remember just what else it destroys, but I do know it attacks the brain cells."

"Damn," Conek breathed. "How much time does she have?"

"I don't know. The Halmarins are a bit cagey about that. I think she's safe for a few days. But longer and she will slowly become a vegetable. We've got to get her out of there."

CHAPTER 4

Conek wanted to get Gella off Halmarin-IV because he needed her to haul cargo. He *had* to get her off the planet before she was affected by the atmosphere.

He didn't give Andro time to put a lengthening silence to his information before they were on the way out of the restaurant, hurrying to catch the first shuttle to the surface and the spaceport.

When they reached the main surface terminal, Conek headed for a computerized port hopper with Andro following close behind.

"I should work for the government. Then I wouldn't have to stay on the job either," Conek complained, afraid the major's desire to go with him might delay him from leaving Agnar-Alpha. "You don't need to go along."

"You're licensed in Agnar-Alpha, love," Andro retorted. "I'm going along to make sure you don't disrupt diplomatic relations."

Conek gave the major a sour look, ready with a retort of his own. He kept it to himself when he saw the slight twitch at the side of Andro's left eye. He was as interested in diplomacy as he was in the chemical content of Malovian game cards. Despite the authority of his position, he had been deeply involved with a small contingent of the ex-smuggling population of Vladmn. During the recent rebellion, Gella had saved the life of Andro's aunt. He was going out of concern, and, as usual, afraid of the danger that might be waiting but fear never stopped him.

They entered the small port hopper and Conek punched in the destination while Andro closed the door. The small surface craft rolled out of the well-protected tunnel and started across the port.

A grotesque ruin of twisted metal and concrete surrounded the spaceport. It stretched a hundred kilometers into the distance, the ruin of a huge metropolis.

Agnar-Alpha was the seat of government for the tri-galactic space government of Vladmn. Until a hundred years before, the city had been on the surface of the planet. It had been a huge glittering jewel of a complex with the pride of an industrial and financial center as well as the ruling city.

Then meteor storms started pounding the planet as if the first star stones blazed a path and the rest followed on a predetermined course. Agnar-Alpha had moved underground, leaving a vast ruin of twisted metal and stone where the crowded metropolis had been. For the last century the only signs of life on the surface were a few fast-growing crops and the spaceport.

Because of the meteor storms, all the space vessels using Agnar-Alpha for their home port had to be sheltered. Kilometers of hangars lined the rows of landing pads, their fantastically tall, steeply pitched roofs rose in concave curves to sharp ridges. From the air they resembled sword blades.

Conek's own fleet of freighters was made up of four huge Osalt ships he had stolen from the enemy federation and a huge alien ghoster he had salvaged. The only shelters large enough to hold his vessels were unused government hangars at the far end of the spaceport.

He and Andro approached to within a half a kilometer of the cavernous buildings when a flurry of movement caught his attention. More than a dozen robots were zipping around the entrance of a hangar, making dashes out onto the landing pad, picking up something too small to see from half a kilometer away.

But Conek knew what was happening. He pushed the emergency stop button on the hopper.

"We'll walk the rest of the way," he told the major.

"Love, we don't have time for beneficial exercise," Andro groused.

"You'll wish you did, if we run over a slither," Conek snapped. "Those little devils are loose again."

"What—are you shipping animals?" Andro asked, suddenly all attention. Vladmn had strict laws on the transportation of non-sentients between worlds. The metabolic balance of a placid herd animal from one planet could be irritated by the differences in atmosphere or food on another world. Many had been known to turn vicious or develop communicable diseases. Vladmn had paid a high price before the space government enforced the restrictions.

"No, Sis-Silsis's nursery," Conek replied as he watched the smooth plasticrete surface for escapees. "They can slip through a hole too small to let steam out." The last was an impossibility of course, but the slithers were artists at fleeing the nest.

"He should try a little discipline," Andro griped at the delay.

"It's instinct," Conek explained, though he was more irritated than the major. "Until after the plague hit Cargonasse they were still hatched in the wild, where the activity brings some sort of predatory birds. They're born with a need to flee the nest for safety. It can't be trained out of them until they're older—but the next time I hire a pilot, remind me to check—I want him single and impotent."

"Are you setting the example for your employees?" Andro smirked as he followed Conek across the plasticrete landing pad.

Directly ahead they saw a glitter of golden wings coming in their direction. Like it or not, they were on the roundup committee.

"Just shut up and catch as many of the little monsters as you can," Conek said, pointing to a small light gold cynbeth that was making a determined dash for freedom. He loped off in another direction to catch two who were leaping and fluttering their wings, gliding toward the weeds at the edge of the landing area.

Four meters from the edge of the paving Conek made a dash, bending down to swoop up a small blue-gold slither. He lost his balance and fell, banging his knee and then his elbow as he rolled to keep from crushing the little creature he held in his hand.

"Rule one, don't stoop and run at the same time," he muttered, getting to his feet. He continued to mutter, but deliberately kept his tone even, hoping to hold on to his temper. At that particular moment, dropping Sis-Silsis and his brood in a Grevotan slime pit seemed an attractive idea.

His fall had positive results. Two other infant cynbeth had stopped to watch his roll and came fluttering over, barking curiously. Conek took advantage of their interest and grabbed them, tucking the first one under his arm as he held the other two.

Once captured, the little reptiles transferred their attention to him, curling their tails around his arms and chirping.

"Yeah, you're satisfied now that you've had your run," he groused, turning his head to keep the blue-gold from poking its snout in his mouth.

"How often do you go through this?" Andro puffed as he came running up with his captive. "I'd find another pilot if I were you."

"It won't be for much longer," Conek said, looking forward to the time when Sis-Silsis turned his brood over to the care centers on his home planet, but he had already learned the males of the species cared for their young until they were old enough for discipline. He sighed for the time when all he had to worry about was some irate patrol ship on his tail. At the moment his old life seemed to have attractions he had overlooked.

But help was on the way. Speeding toward them, and,

more important, carrying a small plasteel cage, came a small droid. Its blue-gray metal body was roughly human-shaped, approximately the size of a stocky five-year-old child.

Cge, the spelling of his name taken from the markings inside his left arm and pronounced *Kay* by his own insistence, was an alien unit. Like his thirteen larger companions, he had been aboard the Skooler ghoster ship *Windsong* when it crashed on the desert planet of Beldorph nearly two years before. He had been damaged in the crash, and never fully repaired. His occasionally malfunctioning computer had led him to develop some supra-mechanical attitudes, one of which was his fierce attachment to his owner.

"ConekHayden's locomotive joint is malfunctioning?" Unable to tilt his head, Cge bent forward to scan the tear in Conek's pants. The Skooler language was all in musical tones, so the alien droids spoke with inflections that caused them to sound almost human. Yet because their emphasis was not organic, they sounded more alien than Vladmn units.

"Never mind that, let's have the cage," Conek ordered. When they had securely penned the four cynbeth slithers, Andro greeted the small droid.

"Hello, Cge, how are you?"

"All my systems are in order, thank you, do you function correctly, MajorAvvin?" The little droid held out his hand according to the instructions Andro had given him shortly after he was repaired.

Conek turned away from the ceremonial greeting as two of his pilots came trotting down the pavement. The first to reach them was Sis-Silsis, the cynbeth sire of the escaped infants. He peered into the cage, hissed at his offspring, and turned to shout to the rest of the searchers that they had caught them all. He was scarcely more than a meter in length, a reptile whose golden scales glittered in the sun. He was Conek's smallest pilot, and because of the slithers, the most troublesome.

Conek put up with the inconvenience because the cynbeth were natural pilots who could get the most from their ships, understanding to an nth the amount of stress a vessel could take without harm. A not inconsiderable advantage was their sense of loyalty to their friends and kin, but their moral code came to an abrupt halt at that point.

The second pilot was human. Alstansig Lesson was fiftyish, a dry stick of a human who flew another of the Osalt freighters. When the ship was on the ground, he was usually flying off the spirits he liberated from the first bottle he could find and as many as were available or he could afford. At the moment he looked a little unsteady. Since he was scheduled for some downtime Conek didn't mention it.

"Good catch," Lesson said, grinning at Conek. "Little critter must have outweighed you to bring you down like that." He turned to eye Andro suspiciously. Like the rest of Conek's pilots, Lesson was also an ex-smuggler, and his old prejudices still decorated the edges of his mind. "Hello, dolly-boy, what have we done now?"

Conek bit back his grin as he watched Andro bristle.

"Pilot Lesson, I resent—"

"Are we going back to Osalta?" Cge piped up, bending backwards to look up at Conek.

"Osalta?" Conek frowned down at the droid. "Where'd you get that idea?"

Cge's sensor panel blinked rapidly. "When Androthemajor flies with us we—do not ship cargo."

"You mean he only shows up when there's trouble," Lesson said, filling in the droid's explanation. "That's true enough."

"Yeah, and it's trouble," Conek said, explaining about Gella. He hadn't finished his explanation when Sis-Silsis let out a hiss and spread his wings.

"Those shrunken little vermin," Lesson growled. "Load those little critters on board, Sis-Silsis. We'll call in Ister, Skielth, pick up some of the boys on Siddah-II, and give them a taste of—"

"No, you won't, love," Andro interrupted. "You wouldn't get her out, and you'd have the entire Vladmn Patrol on your tails. You can't attack a planet."

"Andro's right—" Conek added but Sis-Silsis, standing with his wings half spread, hissed an interruption.

"S-she has-s one of my s-slithers aboard. Do you think

I'm a four-eyed torch who would leave his hatchlings to those—*humanoids*?" He gave the last word the inflection of a curse.

"You can't land on any Halmarin world," Andro argued. "You know their policy on reptiles."

"They've got my eldest," Sis-Silsis spit out the last word. "He'll be silswissy."

Silswissy meant potent; the infant he was talking about was capable of helping to rebuild the depleted species that had nearly been destroyed by a plague. He was not only important as an offspring of Conek's pilot, but to the entire planet of Cargonasse, and to Vladmn who had worked ceaselessly for the continued existence of the cynbeth species.

"You still can't go," Andro argued. "Think of the rest of your brood. You can't take them. The Halmarins don't consider any reptile sentient."

"They admit we're intelligent enough; they say we're from the dark masters," Sis-Silsis replied. "That we were created to bring evil. There's no telling what they will do to him."

"Then don't keep us here talking," Conek said. "We'll have better luck in getting him out than you will."

"Cynbeth take care of their own," Sis-Silsis argued, picking up the cage that held his young and starting back for the ship.

Conek, Andro, and Lesson accompanied him as they walked toward the hangars, and all three humans put forward arguments for keeping *Destria* and the nursery off the planet of Halmarin-IV.

"But, dear ones, we don't have to convince him to stay away from Halmarin-IV," Andro said suddenly. "If I remember correctly there is some treaty agreement among several of the worlds in that sector, and the law forbids the landing of any reptile on the Halmarin Union of Planets."

"Patrols," the reptile spat, but he pulled in his long thin tongue, a sure sign he didn't want his thoughts known.

"Think about it, love," Andro said. "You could evade the patrols and land in the Halmarin system, but they'd get you when you took off. You'd go straight to Balazaro until the sentencing or until I can straighten it out, and what happens to your other slithers then?"

At the mention of the Vladmn prison planet, Sis-Silsis's eyes flashed and wandered independently as he visualized the consequences.

"Never heard of family accommodations on Balazaro," Lesson added. "Never heard of any cynbeth on guard duty there. Wonder if they'd know how to take care of your little winged worms."

Conek tensed for trouble. No one insulted the cynbeth's brood and got away with it, but Sis-Silsis was too occupied with the trouble on Halmarin-IV to notice.

"And you don't know that some of the younger hatchlings might not be silswissy too," Lesson added. "You were telling me so not an hour ago."

"You can't risk them," Conek said. "Besides, it's probably something we can bring her out of. Easier to pay and get them out without a fight if we can."

It took some talking, but finally Sis-Silsis agreed to let Conek and Andro try. He and Lesson volunteered to split Conek's deliveries so he could devote his time to freeing Gella and the little slither.

At the end of the pad, six huge hangars formed a semicircle. The doors of two were open, allowing a view of the ships inside. *Anubis* and *Destria* were alike; huge, roughly diamond-shaped, with wings that looked ridiculously small and stubby, but each wing threw a shadow that could almost cover a Vladmn freighter. Their gleaming white finishes gave off pale reflections of the walls. The two pair of uncovered cockpit transparencies gave them the look of huge, malevolent beasts, staring down at the puny species walking along the pavement.

Conek took out his multipurpose pocket computer and pushed a button, giving off a signal. The doors to a third hangar slowly opened. The first two ships were reduced in comparative size as *his* ship, the giant *Bucephalus*, was revealed, the growing light reflecting off her gleaming hull.

Her cockpit transparencies were also exposed, giving her

the appearance of an alert watcher. Beneath the cockpit, a series of air intake ducts, necessary for cooling the thrusters in close atmospheres, were open, giving her a threatening snarl. Conek had taken advantage of their position and highlighted them with painted trim so the effect was one of visible threat. By comparison, the other two ships looked almost friendly.

All three had been built in the Osalt Federation. Because of the greater distances between settled planets, the Osalt built giant, multipurpose ships, intended to carry passengers as well as cargo.

Even in Osalta, *Bucephalus* was a Goliath.

Five grav-rev beams served her fifteen massive holds. She had been designed with ten staterooms and a lounge to allow her passengers to travel in luxury. Osalta was a lawless territory, and she had been built with armament equal to a Vladmn battleship.

Years before, Conek and his father Tobard went into Osalta to steal ships after Tobard's vessel had been destroyed. The elder Hayden had taken *Anubis* off her maiden voyage, and had been disgusted when his son chose a giant battered old tramp ship, but Conek had never regretted his choice. For years he had worked on *Bucephalus* until only her designers would have recognized her as an old vessel.

Inside she was as luxurious as her hull promised. She was not only Conek's ship, she was his home. No decorator, Conek owed the pleasing choice of soft beige walls, rich brown carpet, and upholstered loungers to Gella Icor's mother, dead for several years. Memory of the laughing Calwain Icor reminded him of his debt to both Gella's parents and gave him added impetus to protect the girl.

As he strapped Cge into a lounger and headed for the cockpit, his mind raced, trying to form some plan. But it was hard to make a decision when he didn't know what he was facing. He strapped himself into the right seat and waited while Andro took the copilot's position. He intended to ask the major what else he knew about Halmarin, but as the lights of the cockpit brightened, he noticed the fatigue lines around Andro's mouth.

He activated the taxi motors and rolled *Bucephalus* out of the hangar and onto the landing pad. He needed a change of subject to calm his whirling thoughts, something to get his mind off Gella until he could decide on a course of action. Then he remembered a piece of gossip making the rounds of the spaceport.

"Hear you've been taking some advanced training lately," he said as he warmed the thrusters.

"Doesn't hurt to keep up-to-date," Andro said, turning on the copilot's computer and calling up the flight checklist.

"You can't go after him alone," Conek warned, knowing what was in the major's mind.

Andro's left eye started twitching again. His girlish mouth tightened to a hard line. Conek knew why. If he lived two centuries he'd never forget the horror of the broadcast from Delevort. During the rebellion, the monster killer, Onetelles, had decimated the population of Quinta Norden's and Andro's ancestral planet while trying to get information on the quinta. A Vladmn Patrol had landed and had broadcast the full story of the carnage. Andro had sworn to destroy Onetelles himself.

"They still haven't found but six hundred survivors," the major said sadly. "That devil's out there, and I'm going to be the one to get him."

"Any news?" Conek asked as he watched the screens, waiting for the warming thrusters to reach operating temperature.

"Nothing, but he's out there."

"When are you leaving?"

"Leaving?" Andro's eyes widened. His surprise would have been convincing to most people.

"Don't try to pull an act on me," Conek warned. "You're just waiting until you can get one of the new CD-35-As. They'll be coming off the production line anytime now."

The major's surprise was genuine. Then he turned caustic. "Any other classified information you want to admit knowing?"

"No, but I'll give you some little known data. If you slip off and Onetelles doesn't kill you, I'll break your neck. You can have the main portion, but I want a *piece* of him."

Andro didn't answer. Conek raised the ship and comped too close to the planet. They grayed with the objections of one of Andro's port authority men fading out with the clarity of normal space.

Back in the lounge, Conek picked up the subject of the argument on the landing pad.

"I don't trust Sis-Silsis," he told Andro as he unstrapped Cge from a seat and helped the little unit to the floor.

"Then why did you hire him?"

"I'd trust him with my life, my ships, and my business, but not to stay out of this. He wants his kid back."

"He could cause an inter-territorial incident," Andro frowned. "I'll have the patrols keep an eye on him."

"You can forget that," Conek said as he walked over to the bar and poured two mild drinks. He wanted to keep his head clear and Andro looked as if a stiff drink would knock him out.

"You don't like the idea?" The major's eyes turned dark. Below the surface of their friendship, Andro never forgot he was an officer in the Vladmn Patrol or that Conek and all his hired pilots had once been wrong-side runners.

Conek shrugged. "Do it if you want, but it's a waste of manpower. There's not a patrol pilot in the territory that could keep up with that slippery little lizard if he wanted to escape. The only time they could catch him is when he lifted off Halmarin-IV."

"After the damage is done," Andro muttered.

"Yeah. And just by going he could cause the death of both Gella and his slither."

CHAPTER 5

One mild drink was enough to knock Andro off his feet. He took advantage of the staterooms to catch up on his sleep. While the ship was in time-comp, Conek sat at the library console he had installed in the lounge and added to his knowledge of the Halmarin Union of Planets.

"Humph, they originally came from Earth," he muttered. Nothing in his information bank accounted for the Halmarin's loss of size. "I wonder if it was something on the planet that affected the genes of the first settlers. Something caused them to shrink—maybe something in the atmosphere," he said aloud while he ran back over the information.

"Will you get smaller if you land on the planet?" Cge asked.

Conek swiveled his chair to discover the little droid had been reading over his shoulder. Behind Cge were Lovey-I and Lovey-II, two of the large worker droids that had been aboard the Skooler ghoster Conek had claimed and repaired. They stood just under two meters tall, their shapes were contoured to give them more of a human shape than Cge's. The lights behind their sensor panels pulsed slower than Cge's, and their computers were not as rapid in processing data. Every time Conek gave them an order, he dredged up a new irritation at Andro for giving them those ridiculous names.

"Maybe *you* will," Conek retorted. He had never accepted Cge's ability to take a random comment and carry it into the hypothetical. He knew what gave Cge the abilities that often caused his owner problems. After the little unit was nearly destroyed the Vladmn roboticists had been unable to attach the replacement parts directly and had been forced to keep some of his damaged Skooler panels. As a result some of his computations were skewed, but the little droid was still supposed to be a machine. Cge seemed to have forgotten it.

Cge stood scanning him as if working out the information. Then he gave three rapid blinks and turned to the larger units. He tilted backward until he nearly lost his balance as he whistled imperiously. Lovey-I and II backed up, whistling back their objections.

"I told you before, speak Vladmn," Conek demanded, wondering what order Cge had given the workers. He knew those three rapid blinks. They always proceeded something unexpected, often trouble.

"It is not logical to send us down on Halmarin-IV," Lovey-II, the more voluble of the two, answered. "If we are reduced in size, we will be less effective to our design."

"Damn it, Cge!" Conek frowned at the little droid, but he had been caught flat-footed. How was he to order the little scamp not to tease the larger units, when Cge had used Conek's own joke?

"Sometimes you're just too smart," he grumbled and shut off the information bank. A glance at his chronometer warned him they would soon be coming back into normal space in the Halmarin solar system.

"One, scratch up some food, Two, you get the major up and in here. Before long we've got people to meet. Tell him I need him alert and charming in case we need to be convincing."

Minutes later Andro came stumbling into the lounge, but he had nothing to say until he had downed two cups of feine and had finished off a prepackaged meal.

He followed Conek into the cockpit as the alarm warned them that they were coming out of time-comp.

No one in Vladmn really understood time-comp. The system had been discovered on an alien ghoster before Conek was born. While the Vladmn construction computers could duplicate it, not even they could explain it, or the advanced mathematical concept on which it was designed. For years theories had bounced back and forth over the steepled fingers of theoretical physicists, but they had never succeeded in adding to the alien system or adapting it for any other related use.

When the gray of time-comp gave way to normal space, they were looking out on a solar system where the six of the nine planets had a strange uniformity of color. They were all a dull brown.

"I hope they gain something as we approach," Andro said. "Ugly isn't an adequate word."

"I'd never heard they were the beauty spots of the galaxy," Conek said. "Is that crud atmosphere?"

Most settled planets were a combination of blue, green, and swirling white. It usually took a combination of water, plant life, and air currents to create a habitable environment. But anything was possible, Conek decided.

"Company coming," he said as a converted freighter appeared out from behind a small asteroid. The ship was old, a patched-up Franig system freighter, obsolete a century before.

"No identification—at least none visible," Andro said, using a tight-beam, distance-scanning sensor. "Tell your old friends we're not worth boarding."

"That's not a smuggler." Conek checked the charges in his forward ship blasters.

"Sorry, I forgot," Andro retorted, sounding edgy. "They always have carefully forged registrations, prominently displayed."

"Yeah," Conek answered. He didn't take offense. The major had a habit of turning snappy when he was worried and tense. "They're either independent pirates or—"

Above his head the communications speaker chattered as a message came through, warped and garbled because the sender was off-band, a common problem with old, poorly serviced equipment.

"At least they want to talk." Conek adjusted the sensor to make up for the deficiency. The voice was all outraged civil authority.

"*Repeat, reply at once or we will open fire.*"

Conek flipped the sending switch, identifying himself and his ship. "Our destination is Halmarin-IV. We're on a diplomatic mission and carry no cargo." He added the last in case he had misjudged the voice and the stranger was a pirate after all.

"I am Commander Arsel, of the Halmarin Benevolent Aid and Peace Assistance Authority. By my order you will add to the information already given, a complete list of personnel and passengers aboard your ship. Failure to comply or a false report will result in severe penalties."

Conek decided he didn't care much for the Halmarin personality if this character was any example, but he held his temper.

"I have three mechanicals aboard and one passenger, Major Andro Avvin."

Silence followed. Conek was just reaching for the switch to ask if his last message was received when the speaker crackled again.

"Major Avvin is a member of the Vladmn Patrol," the officious officer informed them.

"He's here in an unofficial capacity," Conek argued, but the colonel ignored him.

"Halmarin maintains its autonomy. No member of the Vladmn Patrol may land without prior permission. If you wish to return without him, you will be allowed to land with your mechanicals, but they may not leave the ship."

Conek flipped the off switch on the communicator and turned to Andro. The major seemed disappointed but not surprised.

"You didn't expect to be allowed to land," he accused the major.

"It was worth a try," Andro sighed. "It might have worked."

"*What* might have worked?"

"Once I was on the planet, I could have charged Gella on suspicion of smuggling. Since Vladmn claims supersede local law, I could have taken her off world."

"But they *knew* that! *I* knew that! Every settled planet in all three galaxies knows it! I thought you had something better in mind. I ought to drop you on the nearest asteroid—"

"Not the nearest, love. About eight back," Andro corrected him. "The sector patrol station. It won't take you more than three hours to drop me off and return."

Conek gritted his teeth, activated the communicator again, and gave Commander Arsel his returning E.T.A. It galled him to be so cooperative, but showing his feelings would not help Gella.

Less than three hours later he was in landing orbit over Halmarin-IV after having left Andro at the sector patrol station.

And he was convinced he had another problem.

Andro had accepted the Halmarin's refusal to allow him to land with a philosophic attitude at odds with his concern and loyalty to Gella.

"He's up to something," Conek muttered as *Bucephalus* spiraled down toward the landing pad.

"Androthemajor is up to something," Cge repeated from his place in the copilot's seat. "Androthemajor is Gella's friend. Cge is Gella's friend."

Conek frowned at his smallest droid. Cge's use of Vladmn Standard was influenced by Conek's slang. When the little unit used full names instead of pronouns, he was upset, and experience had taught Conek that Cge was capable of making plans of his own.

"You've got something in what serves for *your* mind too. While I'm on Halmarin-IV you're not to leave this ship, or use the communicator. That's an order."

"Cge is not to leave the ship or use the communicator," the droid repeated. The inflection from his speaker was grudging, but not enough to satisfy his owner.

"Lovey-I and II aren't to leave either."

"They will obey," Cge answered.

After more than a year of associating with Cge, Conek knew better than to take the droid's assurance at face value. By association and experience he'd programmed his own deviousness into the little mechanical, and often found it used against him.

"They'll obey you. You are not to ask, suggest, or order them to leave this ship."

Cge turned his sensor module away, giving Conek a view of the back of his head.

"Don't turn stubborn on me. Repeat what I said!"

Half an hour later *Bucephalus* was sitting on the landing pad of Halmarin-IV's capital city. He had carefully chosen his words in ordering Cge to do nothing. He had changed his clothing, putting on one of his see-how-respectable-I-am outfits. Still, when he left the ship, he was uneasy.

Gella had too many friends, all ready to jump in and save her, and that might be her greatest danger. With Lesson, Sis-Silsis, Andro, and now Cge ready to start trouble on her behalf, he knew the problem was moving from simmer to boil, and he wasn't sure he could keep the lid on it.

From space Halmarin-IV had appeared to be an experiment in desolation. Once he'd reached the surface, Conek decided he liked it better from a distance.

The crud was atmosphere, or the atmosphere was crud, a toss-up. Apparently the local vegetation lacked chlorophyll, or it had mutated, because even the plants were brown. Brown hills, valleys, roads—they were hard-tamped earth—brown sludgy streams, all nature on Halmarin-IV was colorless.

Maybe that was why the Halmarins were crazy about color, he decided. To make up for their drab world, they went in for bludgeoning primary colors that slammed against the senses. They interspersed them with glaring pinks, greens, and purples that seemed to glow, spearing and holding the attention as if pinning it to a wall.

Commander Arsel had kept his promise and waited at the asteroid. He not only led Conek to the spaceport, but landed and escorted the captain to a huge, bright, mustard-colored building in the center of the capital city.

The commander led the way down a hall, bustling with the officiousness of an unimportant cog in a large machine.

Conek's hopes rose as he was passed beyond bulwarks of receptionist and secretarial types and ushered into a large imposing office. He walked across an expanse of bright green carpet to stand in front of an orange desk and greet Citizen Charno-vins, Minister of Justice.

Conek was surprised. He had expected to be brought before the customs officials. He decided they took their embargo laws seriously.

Behind the desk, the little man in the red and mustard tunic regarded him silently. The minister looked to be elderly, though it was hard to tell the age of a Halmarin. Conek made his judgment based on the wrinkles dissecting the folds of extra skin that hung on his face like an oversize garment.

"Thank you for seeing me so promptly," Conek said, trying for his friendliest smile. "You are no doubt aware that your patrol has taken one of my pilots in custody."

The minister nodded, disturbing his jowls that dribbled folds of skin.

"One Gella Icor. I am aware of it."

"If there was something in her cargo that's illegal in the Halmarin Union, we shipped it in ignorance. We are more than willing to pay any compensation for the inconvenience."

One reason shippers weren't notified of sudden bans was to enable officials to accept bribes to free the offenders. Conek had learned to accept it as an occupational expense. He was sure the cranas he left behind would never find their way into the national treasury.

Then he got his second surprise as the minister seemed offended, shook his head, and looked away from the crana chips in Conek's hand as if the freighter captain might be holding some sort of offal.

"I have no knowledge of any illegal shipment."

"You mean you're holding her for some other reason?" He silently cursed Gella, who had her father's quick temper and talent for getting into trouble.

"For murder," Charno-vins said matter-of-factly.

Conek stared at him, not sure he had heard correctly.

"Gella?" His voice was hoarse with disbelief. "There's got to be some mistake. She'd have a hard time killing in self-defense."

"Dansiz Icor committed the crime," the minister said as if his explanation settled the matter, but it left Conek more confused than ever.

"I knew her father for years, and I can't believe that either—Icor wasn't the type." He'd forgotten all about smiling. "And even if he did, he's dead—dead for almost two years."

"We are aware of that also." Charno-vins nodded and set his loose skin in motion again. "So his daughter will pay his penalty for him."

Conek wondered if he was going space-happy. "But she's not *guilty*!"

"Of course she is," the minister softly insisted, his voice quiet and soothing as if calming a child. "The stain of his guilt is on all those who carry his blood. Her death will cleanse it, leaving those of her line innocent and free."

"That's not going to help a hell of a lot, since she's the last," Conek said, no longer caring if he was insulting or not.

"Better her descendants remain unborn than live under the shadow of his crime. It is our way, what our religion teaches us."

Charno-vins kept his voice and manner friendly, a simple explanation of fact, and Conek found his calm assurance more threatening than if he had ranted and screamed.

His concern over Gella had almost made him forget about his second concern. Belatedly he remembered she had a companion with her.

"And the infant cynbeth? What about it?"

The minister's face hardened. "We do not allow reptiles in the Halmarin Union of Planets. At the moment the creature is alive, since our patrol didn't know what to do about it and considered it some sort of pet. When the sentence is carried out, the creature will be put to death also."

"It's a sentient infant!" Conek protested. "And it has nothing to do with any of this!"

"It came with her and she must pay for her father's crime," the minister reiterated. His wrinkled lips unfolded in a smile. "It's unfortunate that we must inconvenience you by removing one of your pilots, but perhaps we can make it up to you by offering you some hauling contracts. This little incident should not be allowed to create bad feeling."

Oh, hell no, Conek thought. *Just kill a young girl and one of Sis-Silsis's brood for a crime they had nothing to do with, but let's stay friends*!

He kept his face blank. He had faced Vladmn Patrols, hired assassins, and irate commanders of warships determined to blow him out of space, but religious insanity was something else again.

CHAPTER 6

There were more than a million majors in the Vladmn Patrol, but relatively few were based in Agnar-Alpha. Still fewer socialized with the administrative staff that gave out promotions. Only one was known to have set up a brilliant strategy in the recent rebellion, and only one was the nephew of a quinta.

When Conek returned to Ruvor Asteroid, the sector patrol station, he found Andro installed in the most opulent of the V.I.P. quarters, usually reserved for the general staff or planetary dignitaries.

But the station was a small one and the office that had been loaned to Andro was far smaller than his own on Agnar-Alpha. He slammed his chair back against the wall as he pushed himself away from the desk and stood up.

"It's barbaric! We left that nonsense behind centuries before the first human went into space."

"Obviously some of us didn't," Conek said. "The point is, how do we keep those religious fanatics from executing Gella?"

Andro shook his head. "I could *kill* Icor for putting her in this danger," he said.

"First, you're a little late. Two years. Second, Icor didn't do it. That's one thing I'm sure of."

"Why?"

"Someone burned down more than a dozen unarmed miners who were traveling down a backcountry road. The story is they saw a ship land. Thinking it was in trouble they went to play assistance and rescue. Two of them made it back alive."

"What tied it to Icor?"

"The freighter was an old CD-51. It carried his registration number."

"So what makes you so sure it wasn't Icor?"

"Because I *knew* him. He'd never have a reason. He wasn't a criminal—" That made a lot of sense. "What I mean is, he only went so far across the line. If the patrols had caught him the most they could have charged him with was evading customs. What is the worst he could have expected?"

Andro shrugged. "Evading customs—three to six months—maybe only a fine, depending on the cargo."

"Not enough to kill for," Conek said. "He didn't deal in addictives or slaves. I never knew him to sell illegal weapons. Nothing he did was worth murder to keep from getting caught."

"You're fabricating a defense."

"I knew Icor. He wasn't guilty."

Andro sat down, folded his hands, and gazed at the ex-smuggler across the desk.

"What do we do about it?"

"There's only one way to save Gella. To find out who *did* kill those miners."

Yeah, the words sounded good, but how did he go about finding one unregistered ship among the millions in the Vladmn Territory? The ship could be a pirate vessel, flying out of the thousands of uncharted asteroid bases. It would be easier to fit Skielth in a cynbeth skin.

"Just tell me how and I'll go do it." Andro sounded as skeptical as Conek felt.

But just thinking of Skielth, his big Shashar friend, gave Conek an idea.

"Can you catch a ride back to Agnar-Alpha?"

Andro's eyes narrowed. "What are you going to do?"

"Ask some questions—and if I get the answers you can't afford to hear them."

Conek waited while the major worked that one out. In the recent rebellion Andro had learned the value of being able to call on the smugglers of Vladmn, but his position would not allow him to overlook blatant lawbreaking. He was caught between officialdom and expediency.

"I'll get back to Agnar-Alpha," he said slowly. "The commander here needs to shuttle a couple of ships back to Chalson-Minor for servicing. I could take one and get a lift back from there. Can I have Lovey-I for a copilot?"

"Only if you stay out of trouble. No chasing Onetelles with him aboard."

"I wish there was a chance," Andro sighed. "And don't stay away too long. *I* can't stop Lesson and Sis-Silsis before they land on Halmarin-IV.

"Oh, there's another problem," Andro said. "Those magnetic flare-ups are due soon. They'll ground most flights in that area."

"We'll have her out by then," Conek assured the major. He hoped he was right.

On his way to his ship and halfway across the galaxy, Conek congratulated himself on having gotten rid of Andro so easily. He kept trying to ignore that niggling little critter walking on his backbone.

Added to his irritation was the way the two droids still kept watching him. When they followed him across the lounge for the fourth time in one hour he turned, his patience at an end.

"All right! You've looked long enough! Have I shrunk any?"

"We have not yet noted a reduction in your height," Lovey-II answered him. "We will continue to monitor," the big droid added as if Conek could take comfort from their attention.

"Go measure each other, you were down there too, even if you didn't leave the ship." He strode toward the cockpit, angry with himself for losing his temper with the droids and wondering what he might be doing to their systems with his threats. Just before he left the lounge he looked back. Lovey-II and Cge were scanning each other carefully. That would keep them busy, he thought. He was wrong. Cge was following him before he could get more than a few steps away.

"Androthemajor will not shrink," Cge said. "He did not go down on the planet."

"No, he's on his way back to Agnar-Alpha, and if I'd thought about it I would have sent you two with him," Conek groused.

"But he was not returning to Agnar-Alpha," Cge said. "He went to Newhouse."

"What?" Conek stared down at the little droid. The Newhouse system was the third planet colonized by Earth, hundreds of years before. It had degenerated into a lawless melting pot of transients, pirates, and independent smugglers who'd ship anything for a price. It was also open to the Vladmn Patrol, but once on any of the three planets in the system, every individual was on his own.

No one in his right mind went to Newhouse. Certainly not the prim and fastidious administrator of the Agnar-Alpha port authority.

"You've got a loose connection. He wouldn't go there—and if he did, he wouldn't tell you about it."

"He did not tell me," Cge piped. "You commanded me not to speak on the communicator. You did not forbid listening."

Conek's backbone critter broke into a sprint. "Exactly what did you hear?"

"Just before you returned, he ordered a ship turned over to him—a CC-12. I lack data on that type of vessel."

"It's an old heap, probably one of the oldest in space. He must have been desperate to get back to work," Conek mused. "I probably should have taken him."

"But why would he request the coordinates of Newhouse to be loaded in the flight computer if he was returning to Agnar-Alpha?"

"He wouldn't, and I'd better get to Skielth fast," Conek growled. "We'll need all his hatchling peers to keep that idiot from getting killed." As if he didn't have enough trouble trying to get Gella out of danger.

Conek wished they could take their problems one at a time.

CHAPTER 7

"A cheap little pill to ruin a thousand-crana drunk!" Skielth stared down at the little capsule in his webbed and clawed hand.

"But you'll take it," Histilsia ordered, her blue-green tail switching. "If it had not been for Gella Icor, you might not be here now, and I'll content myself with that until your return."

Conek grinned up at the large Shashar female, glad she was understanding about having her bridegroom pulled away from her less than four hours after the wedding ceremony. The females of the Shashar were as large as the males and reputed to be twice as fierce in a fight.

Snatching her mate out of her own home could be upsetting—if this place could be thought of as home, he amended as he stepped quickly aside to avoid a fine spray of water that sprang up out of the moss-covered floor.

The Shashar house was built entirely of green-tinted, transparent acrilosteel. The floor was natural earth, carpeted by living moss, and the walls were ringed with what appeared to be an impenetrable wall of plants, many of the bottom leaves a meter wide. In the main room of the house four trees, thin-boled but with heavy thick foliage, kept out most

45

of the sun's rays. The only furnishings were small pedestal tables, low by Shashar standards, but hip high on Conek. Since the reptiles of the planet sat on their tails, there were no chairs.

The huge reptiles had begun life and development in the hot swamplands near the equator of their planet. After they achieved their technology they scorned the swamps that bred them and moved to the cooler, more arid lands. They still liked heat and moisture, so they re-created within their houses the rain forests they had left behind.

Conek dodged another spray of water and in doing so stepped under one of the trees. He accidentally brushed one of the lower branches and a shower of water went down his neck.

It had been a bad day all around, he thought.

Conek had checked MD-439 and Siddah-II before discovering Skielth had returned to his home planet, and when Conek arrived on the reptilian planet he walked into a party Shashar style, complete with enough inebriating spirits to float a small star ship.

He had been cursing his bad luck in not being able to find Skielth, but when he arrived he knew the trip had been more than worth the trouble. Besides being reptile, the Shashar shared with the cynbeth the trait of loyalty. Other smugglers might turn on a competitor of the same species, but the Shashar believed in live and let live among their own kind and a debt owed by one was often recognized by other Shashar.

Seven of Skielth's contrabanding friends were present at his wedding, and they had all accepted one of the Anacan-made capsules that would destroy the glow of the liquor they had consumed.

While Conek watched, the Shashars' eyes lost the blue glow that showed inebriation in the species. Their expressions showed little to the average human, but by the movement of their long tongues and the shaking of their heads, they were going through their hangovers at light speed. A Shashar bolt was strong enough to send a human flying without his ship, and they'd been at it for hours.

Skielth shook his head one final time and gave a deep grumble before he focused his eyes on Conek.

"Halmarin," he muttered. "What would a smuggler want in that sector? Nothing there."

"There has to be something," Conek said. "The CD was on the ground, the Halmarin miners went to offer help and got burned for it. Someone was keeping something a secret. The only way to get Gella out of there is to find out what and who."

"No chance of just flying in there and breaking her out? Can't we just break her out?" Jussislin, a younger, thinner Shashar, asked. He had a trick of repeating himself when addressing anyone other than his own kind.

"Don't think I wouldn't," Conek said, "but we don't know where she's being held."

"No chance of bribing some official?" Skielth asked.

"Not a chance. They're religious fanatics. They believe they're doing Gella a favor. Better that she dies than live with Icor's guilt staining her soul."

"They hate reptiles too," Georvis added as if that was the final proof of their insanity.

"Could they be right about Icor?" Jussislin asked Skielth, and soon learned his mistake.

"When you've been through several more sheddings, you'll learn better than ask stupid questions," Skielth roared. "Icor was my friend." He glared at Jussislin until the younger reptile lowered his chin, tapping it against his chest in mute apology.

"Take it as a given, Icor did not burn those humanoids," Skielth announced to the ring of reptiles surrounding Conek. "If he had, we wouldn't be asking who did do it, we'd be on our way to Halmarin-IV to blast his daughter out."

"We're still left with the question of what a smuggler would be doing in that area," Georvis reminded them.

"I'd guess it's slaves or addictives," Conek said. "It's something they don't get from Tsaral's network." He looked around and saw the confusion on several reptilian faces, but Skielth beat him to the explanation.

"If they got their goods through Tsaral, we'd know about their ship."

"Maybe they'd be around sometime," Jussislin spoke up, anxious to get back in Skielth's good graces again. "They could have another registration number—just bolting it on over Icor's when they didn't want it seen."

"That's an idea," Conek said, skipping to the side, but not in time to avoid another sudden spray of water. That one had been higher. He took it straight in the face.

"We'll spread out around the sector and see what we can pick up," Skielth said. Then he looked Conek up and down. "You look like a half-drowned Orelian." The flesh on his dorsal ridge rippled and his wide mouth stretched in a smile. The ripple was the natural movement of humor among the Shashar. The smile was artificial, a learned expression to let Conek know the reptile was making a joke. "You get back to your ship and dry off, though why all you humanoid species want to wear clothing beats me."

Conek wondered too as he trudged back to his ship. While in the Shashar house he had been wanting to get back outside into a cooler, dryer atmosphere, but when he left evening was advancing and with it the surface temperature had turned from pleasantly cool to cold. The slight wind turned his wet clothing icy cold.

"I wish to hell you had gone instead of me," he yelled at Cge who had turned sulky when he found out he was to be left on the ship, but the little droid forgot his injuries when he saw his master's wet clothing.

Back on Agnar-Alpha, Conek found Lesson and Ister in the lounge on *Anubis*. Luckily, Sis-Silsis had taken off earlier that day with a rush shipment to Kirbonil in the Beta Galaxy.

"They wouldn't even let her have a breather massk?" Ister hissed the last word after Conek told the two pilots what he had learned on Halmarin-IV.

"I tried to leave some, but they wouldn't take them," Conek said. "We've got to get her out, and fast."

"Icor wouldn't have done it," Lesson said, as if he were

the only one of the dead smuggler's friends to believe it. "If the truth were known, he was probably drinking on Siddah-II when the Halmarins were burned."

"If we could prove that—" Ister said, but Conek cut him off.

"If we could find the ship, we might get the answer in his logs," Conek said, and jumped to his feet, running his fingers through his short blond hair in his agitation. "Why didn't I think of that when I was there?"

"Even if you had, we couldn't access them," Lesson objected.

"But Gella could," Conek broke in. "Maybe I'm hoping too much, but if I get on to that Halmarin fanatic and explain, they might be willing to let us prove it."

"You think they'd listen to reason?" Ister was doubtful.

"I think I know how to approach it so they can't refuse," Conek said, rising and starting for the passenger lift at the front of the lounge.

"Oh, before you go, you've got an urgent message," Lesson said, going to the cockpit and bringing back a plastic strip for Conek to insert into his hand computer.

Conek pulled out his pocket unit and inserted the strip, knowing it was too early to expect to hear from Skielth, but perhaps Andro had found out something. He read the message and grunted in disgust. Lagon Fellerd was demanding to know why his shipment of precidine wasn't delivered to Vilarona on schedule.

"So the next time it rains he can let his units wear plastic sheets," Conek muttered. Waterproofing for mechanicals couldn't be considered a priority when Gella's life was at stake.

In minutes he was back on *Bucephalus* and had arranged for an inter-spacial call to Halmarin-IV. His comm-unit on the ship could have reached the planet, but some backwater planets still demanded communication come through government channels. He was drumming his fingers on the edge of the control panel in the cockpit when the port authority sergeant who was placing the call picked up the connection with Conek again.

"I'm sorry, Captain Hayden, but this Halmarin Minister of Justice won't accept a call from you."

"Well, just who will he accept a call from?" Conek demanded, thinking Charno-vins might be using the issue to get on speaking terms with some authority on Agnar-Alpha. Never mind that Gella's brain could be turning to jelly, politics came first.

Sergeant Kacklac left the ban again but was back within a minute. "He's not accepting any calls from off planet, sir."

"Then get me someone that is, or I'll come down there and pull your ears off, Sergeant!"

"Captain Hayden, you will leave the sergeant's ears alone."

Conek blinked as a new voice intruded into the conversation. He recognized it as Quinta Norden's. Most private citizens in the tri-galactic territory would have been honored to speechlessness even to receive a reprimand from one of the five top officials in the government, but Conek had had too many run-ins with Norden to be daunted.

"What is the job description of a quinta, Quinta? Gella is in trouble, and I've got no time for official protocol."

"Gella is my friend too," Norden reminded him. "If I thought it would help I'd risk a PME, but all it would accomplish would be to get a lot of patrol members and Halmarin citizens killed, and would certainly bring on Gella's death."

Conek felt like saying she was safe in making noises as long as she had good reasons not to carry through on her statement, but he knew she was right. Religious fanatics would die by the thousands and glory in it.

But Norden was concerned. She asked several questions, and didn't argue or scoff when Conek insisted Icor had not killed the Halmarins.

". . . And her best chance is for us to find out who did," Conek finished.

"You'll be going into some lawless territory," she mused, her voice soft over the comm-link. "I'll send you something that might help. Don't leave Agnar-Alpha until Lieutenant Marwit arrives."

Conek made a noncommittal sound and flipped off the switches on the communicator. He didn't have time to mess around with officials. If Marwit, the handsome head of the quinta's personal guard, arrived before he was ready to leave, fine. If not, he wouldn't wait around.

When Conek left the cockpit he found Ister and Lesson in the lounge on *Bucephalus*. Lesson had printed out a graphic map of the Halmarin area of space and they were ready for a council.

"Why didn't they just take it to their main spaceport?" Ister asked. "Most planets would."

"They're confiscating it, but they don't want to admit it," Lesson said. "So they've hidden it away until the noise dies down, and then they'll modify it, repaint it, and figure no one will know the difference."

"And we'll have a devil of a time finding it," Conek said. They settled down to the complicated task of mapping out a search plan.

They had hardly begun when Lieutenant Marwit arrived with a package he tried to hide from the others. Conek took it, sent the officer back with a message of thanks, and went back to his plans. He tossed the quinta's secret package on a lounger and forgot it for the time being.

When they finished, Lesson and the Orelian went back to their ships and Conek fired the thrusters on *Bucephalus*. He didn't tell them his plans.

Orser, a small planet in the Alpha FarArm, vied with Newhouse for the worst reputation in the sector. It wasn't a place he wanted to go, but with Andro at Newhouse, it was the second best place to check for a CD that might hide its markings.

CHAPTER 8

"Your identity and registration?" The request for information by the Newhouse flight controller was phrased like a question, but it was a demand. If not answered, Major Andro Avvin had already been warned that he could be blown out of space.

Andro felt his brain go numb. He grabbed for the plastene printout card propped up against the thruster firing switches on the control panel.

"Wroger Carls, licensed out of Almiror, ship's registration number DA-190-CC-75934-75," he read from the card and laid it down again while he corrected the erratic course of the old CC-12. He hoped Captain Ergsol on Chalson-Minor was right, that the port authority on Newhouse never bothered to check on the registrations of incoming ships.

If the captain had misled him, Ergsol would find himself assistant to the shovelers on a refuge scow—if Andro got back to take his revenge.

"You're cleared to land," the voice came out of the communit speaker behind his head.

"My landing pad number and direction?" Andro asked.

"Pick one. Hell, you can see what's free better than I can," the flight controller griped. "Maybe they hold your hand on Almiror, but here, if you can't land it you got no business flying." He had hardly quit speaking before the drone of the speaker indicated he had left that frequency or switched off his unit.

Andro flipped off his own speaker and swore.

"Mistake number one," he said to the big dark droid that sat in the copilot's seat. "I should have known they don't run a proper port."

"It is possible for you to instruct them," Lovey-I said. "It is your function."

"You don't repeat that," Andro answered as he eased the old freighter down into the atmosphere. "You remember I'm supposed to be Wroger Carls, a freighter pilot."

"Affirmative. *I* did not forget." The droid's slight emphasis on the personal pronoun served to remind Andro that he had allowed his alias to slip his mind momentarily. The knowledge worried him enough to justify it.

"I wouldn't have if I hadn't been busy trying to keep this ox cart on course!"

"I am to remember the ship is an ox cart," Lovey-I replied, obedient to the rules of their duplicity as Andro had previously explained them.

The old CC-12's computers were in excellent working order, but the sublight speed tracking needed recalibrating, and Andro was busy trying to keep the ship on course. By the time he had explained his slang to the droid and had brought the ship down over the landing area of the main spaceport, he was beginning to wish he had returned to Agnar-Alpha and left the search for Gella's CD-51 to Conek and his pilots.

"And why I bought Hayden's story about Icor's innocence, I don't know," he told Lovey-I. "And don't give me an explanation, because I don't want to hear it."

The port below him was crowded with ships, most of them old, scarred with time and hard service. To his fastidious eye he seemed to be looking down on a space junkyard. The CC-12 should fit right in.

Half an hour later he had landed, cut the thrusters, and given Lovey-I his orders. The droid was to keep the view screens opaqued and not allow entry into the ship by anyone but Andro.

He changed into a set of rusty blue pants and tunic that was well worn, torn on one cuff, and stained on one leg with a few drops of paint. The paint had been added on Chalson-Minor where the Vladmn Patrol ship servicers had given the vessel a quick but expert camouflage and the fictitious registration number.

There were times when it was advantageous to be a relative of a quinta. It didn't hurt his cause to let them know he was working unofficially to help save Gella Icor. Many of them remembered her from the rebellion.

He paused long enough to practice speaking in a lowered, slurred voice that would never fool a voice analyzer, but might get him by on Newhouse. Most of the pilots from that area never strayed onto the Holton/Beta side of Alpha Galaxy and stayed as far away from the center of the Vladmn Patrol area as they could get.

Satisfied that he could pass as a rogue pilot looking for another ship to replace the CC-12, he left the ship and set out for the colored, dancing lights in the center of the ring of landing pads.

The sun had been setting when he landed, and since Newtown, the spaceport on Newhouse, was located near the equator, the twilight had been short. In addition to his blaster, he had clipped a small illuminator to his belt. A small portion of the landing area was paved, and since it was close to Newtown, all the spaces had been taken. Most of the ships were parked on bare earth that had been burned and fused by thruster fire, but patches of it were still soft, and a recent rain had turned it into mire.

"Ugh." Andro stepped in a soft, slimy area that smelled of lubricating fluid. He hurriedly stepped aside and put one hand on the landing support of a Hidderan winger while he scraped the goo from his boots.

"Not your kind of place, I take it," said a voice out of the darkness.

Andro looked around, raised his illuminator, and flashed it in the direction of the voice, but if there was anyone close by, he was either inside the winger or behind one of the supports.

"Augh, one place's as good as another, but I'll not be liking to ruin me last pair of boots," he grumbled, keeping his voice low and dropping all affectation.

"Them as knows Newhouse knows how to keep out of the soft places," the voice came again. The speaker was a simian-type humanoid from the planet Ilchwen, many of the words were pronounced on the inhale, typical of that species. They were most often found on lawless planets. They knew he was a stranger, fair game for mugging and robbery in the dark landing area.

Andro flipped his illuminator to bright and swung it in a wide arc, hoping to momentarily blind the simian who had spoken and any others who might be with him. He backed away from the support leg of the Hidderan winger, reaching for his blaster as he moved.

He wasn't fast enough.

A hairy arm swung briefly across his vision to put an armlock on his throat. With his other hand the apelike humanoid grabbed Andro's wrist to keep him from reaching his blaster.

"Got him," the simian behind him growled.

Andro struggled, and discovered his theory of blinding his opponents worked, at least on the one who had spoken to him. As he came running from cover, Andro was wildly swinging the illuminator, and he did sufficiently destroy the ape's night vision to cause him to run into the winger's support leg. The would-be attacker howled and grabbed his right foot. Simian feet had never taken to boots.

Their feet were vulnerable.

Andro stomped down on the arch of the simian throttling him. The ape released his stranglehold and struck a vicious blow against the major's neck, knocking him to the ground, facedown. He dropped the illuminator and it went rolling across a patch of hard ground. He was reaching for his blaster when a bare foot came down on his hand, the long toes gripping two of his fingers and twisting them back.

His left arm was grabbed and twisted, a hard knee came down in the middle of his back, pressing the breath out of him. In front of him a limping shadow was coming from the darkness under the winger. There were three, he realized as he twisted his head, trying to discover some advantage that would free him before his loss of breath caused him to pass out.

The weight on his back was crushing the breath out of him, and the lights penetrating the darkness were originating in his head when he was blinded by the light of the illuminator and heard the sound of a short burst from a blaster.

"Let him up."

The light was glaring at the simians from nearly two meters off the ground, and they were unable to see what was behind it. Few species were as tall as humans and simians. The Shashar towered over all the others. Simians were usually afraid of the giant reptiles. These backed up, fear in their faces.

Andro was short of breath and not thinking well when the simians released him and stepped back, but he had worked for years in the Vladmn Patrol Service where nearly every species was represented. He recognized the soft clicks behind the translator.

The illuminator was being held by a rrotta, a crustacean whose ancestors had given up the water millennia before. They were long-legged, usually walking with their knees spiked up half a meter over their bodies. This one was extended to his full height.

"Head for that Murrock freighter, and if you try to move out of this beam of light, I'll burn you," the rrotta ordered. "Move it, apes!"

Andro had painfully raised himself to a sitting position, and had started to stand when two of the simians turned their backs on the light and started for the freighter. The limper gave a growl but the flash from a blaster, burning the ground by his feet, convinced him to move after the others.

It also convinced Andro to stay where he was. If his rescuers decided to fire at the simians, he didn't want to be in the way.

But were they saving him or taking over where the apes left off? He moved slowly, stretching as if he were still in pain, and turned his left side toward the illuminator. In the seclusion of the shadow of his right side, he was reaching for his blaster.

"Do not draw your weapon, Major Avvin," a soft voice warned him.

So much for his disguise, he thought. If there were people in Newhouse who recognized him, he would be a dead man within the hour. Frustration made him voice a different complaint. There was no point in trying to disguise his voice if he was known.

"Does everyone on this luck-forsaken planet hide in the shadows to talk?"

"Seemed the thing to do when there was more of them and they were bigger," the rrotta said. "The apes are far enough away. They won't try to sneak back for a while, but we should leave here. Can you walk, Major?"

"I can make it," Andro said, getting to his feet. By the time he was standing the rrotta had turned off the light. Since he had shaded his eyes, he was soon able to see the rrotta's companion was a mentot.

"What now?" Andro asked. He didn't know much about Newhouse, but among what little information he had was that they scorned any law enforcement. These two didn't appear to be the welcome wagon committee.

"We're not here to rob you," the mentot said. "You once helped me. We're repaying the obligation."

They had started walking toward the lights of the spaceport town. When they moved out of the shadow of the winger, Andro squinted, trying to see the meter-long catirpel better.

"Who are you?"

"You wouldn't remember me," the mentot answered.

"A deserter," Andro spoke before he thought. He decided he should get back on his ship and leave. So far he had taken every opportunity to get himself killed. Newhouse was one of the planets where military deserters hid. He knew it and they probably knew he did, but he didn't have to throw it in their faces.

"Not until we had to serve Onetelles." The mentot's translator spat out the name as if it were spewing venom.

"Well, I can't blame you for that," Andro said. "I did

the same thing. Before the rebellion was over, a quarter of the military deserted. There was an amnesty if you had wanted to go back."

"We were on Jolkaar until yesterday," the rrotta said. "By the time we heard we could have gone back, it was too late."

The rrotta had the best night vision and he led them on a zigzag route, keeping to the shadows of the ships. Andro followed and the mentot brought up the rear for the first hundred meters. The major could hear the patti-pat-pat of the mentot's feet as he seemed to be marching double time. Andro remembered mentots had very little night vision. He paused and let the little catirpel take the center position.

"What happens when we get to the spaceport?" he asked. "Are you going to tell your friends who I am?"

"We don't know anyone to tell," the rrotta answered. "You can do what you like."

"I could use some help, and I'm willing to pay for it. I'm after information."

"I hear information can get a person killed on Newhouse," the mentot answered.

"You said you wouldn't serve under Onetelles. Would you help someone who did more to drive out the Amal than anyone else?"

"Someone who did more . . ." the rrotta paused. "Quintas Bentian and Norden . . ."

"The pilot that got them off Agnar-Alpha," Andro interrupted.

"Would Onetelles like to see *her* dead!" The rrotta gave a series of clicks that translated as a chuckle. "Helping her would be a snap at him, even if he didn't know it."

The major gave them the bare bones of Gella's problem. "I'll pay for any information you get for me, and if you want it, I'll see what I can do to get you amnesty."

"You can promise us amnesty?" the mentot asked, his voice full of doubt.

"No promises, I don't know if I can do it." He did know, but his rescuers looked as if they had had a rough time, and weren't ready to trust too confident a statement. There were hundreds, maybe thousands still returning to the military. The original length of time for the amnesty had proven too short for all the deserters to make it back to their stations.

He watched their reactions and knew he had been right in his estimation. While they would have discounted a certainty from him, they accepted the possibility and decided to trust him, giving him their names. The mentot was Nelsf. They had arrived on Newhouse that morning and one of Nelsf's hatching mates, Wiers, was in the spaceport, trying to find accommodation for the three deserters. The rrotta's name was Fsith.

They had deserted their positions in Agnar-Alpha when Onetelles had crippled their sergeant during the search for Quintas Norden and Bentian.

If he was going to trust them, then he shouldn't do it by half measures, Andro decided. He gave them his alias and the cover story he had decided to use.

"I'm hoping to buy another ship, because this one's too old to fly much longer. Something not too new, not too expensive, like a CD, maybe a forty-eight, a fifty-one, or even a sixty-three. Whatever suits my purse."

"Have you got any loading droids?" Nelsf asked.

"No, sold the last ones I had, getting the price together for a new ship," Andro said, answering with the logic of his cover.

"Might need to hire some loaders while you're about it," Fsith, the rrotta, muttered, as if half to himself. "Could take them on without pay until they started to work. If they wanted the job they'd be interested in helping you find a ship."

They were out of money, that was why one of the mentots was scouring the town to find a place to stay—something cheap or free. Hunger had a way of causing people to sell things that didn't fill their stomachs, like honor. If they knew they could stay aboard his ship and eat there, they would be less likely to betray him.

"I just might," Andro agreed. "I might take on three, if they worked for found until I was shipping again."

Newtown reminded Andro of the smugglers' town on Siddah-II, but he would not have said as much to Tsaral. Newtown was older, the buildings shabbier, and a rank vinelike growth grew out of every crack and crevice in the pavement, and up the sides of the walls. Since leaving the ship, he had been conscious of a sickly sweet smell. The vines were the cause.

Most of Newtown's business seemed to be bars, and before they reached the main area, Andro had given his two new employees a few cranas with instructions to spend more of it on food than drink, and to ask their questions openly, depending on their cover to protect them; since they wanted work on his new ship, they were helping him find one.

All the bars were shabby and run-down, so he chose the best one, called the Aerostar, and went in, stepping up to an empty place at the bar. The customers were the usual mixture, with more talovans, simians, txorch, and xrotha than he liked to see in one place. Talovans and simians were always at odds, the xrotha had short tempers, and the txorch just liked to fight.

He wanted to ask some simple questions and leave peacefully, preferably with his head still on his shoulders.

He was still trying to catch the four-eyed jelinian's attention when he felt a touch on his arm. He jumped, startled, though there hadn't been any menace in the brush of one human's arm against another. The man who touched him noticed his abrupt movement and nodded.

"Place looks ripe for trouble," he said softly. "I'd leave, but I'm supposed to meet someone here."

The bartender came around the curve of the bar and put two glasses down, one in front of the stranger and one in front of Andro.

"Drink up," the stranger said, raising his glass. "Looking for someone to talk to while I wait. Name's Starring."

"Wroger Carls," Andro said, glad he had remembered his alias. "On Newhouse looking for a ship."

"It got a name?"

"No, I'm looking to buy something moderately priced and to sell a junker," Andro said. "I want something like an old CD, but in moderately good shape."

"Know of a few around, don't know if they're for sale."

The peace had lasted a full four minutes that Andro knew of, and that was long enough for the txorch. One picked up a bottle, threw it at one of the xrotha. He missed. The bottle thunked against the shoulder of a maned talovan who happened to be standing next to a simian. The talovan roared and knocked the unsuspecting ape flat on his back.

Starring turned to watch the action and nodded.

"Expected it. Grab your drink and follow me." He led the way toward the entrance, but instead of leaving, he pulled out two chairs from a large table that stood in the corner of the room. He crawled under the table, resting his back against the wall.

The last thing Andro wanted was to sit on a filthy floor under a table, but if Starring was in a talkative mood, he might be walking out on his best opportunity. He slid under the table and they watched as one of the apes hit a txorch with a chair and knocked the arthropod over the bar.

"Ten cranas on the txorch," Starring offered.

"I'll take the talovan," Andro answered. He'd lose his money, but he liked the big maned humanoids and Starring might stay friendly if he was making something off Andro.

Behind the bar the jelinian bartender was using three of his eye stalks to watch the fight, and the other to continue serving drinks. He paid no attention to the combatants except to duck a flying mug while he continued to shake a mixer.

"You might ask old Korgal if he wants to sell his CD," Starring said. "It's a sixty-three; needs a little work, but if I had the money I'd take it in a minute."

"You think he wants to sell?"

"Don't know for sure. Then there's Milwin over on Gippin, wanting another ship. His CD-51's in prime condition, but one hold is full of seats. One big atmospheric mixer on it, he's been ferrying passengers between Gippin and Cornstalk for years."

Andro's hopes had risen when Starring had mentioned a fifty-one, but sunk deeper and deeper as Starring continued to talk. He knew of four CD-51s but they were all being flown by legitimate haulers. During the conversation he mentioned his own work, ore freighting. He was only on Newhouse because his ship had developed a guidance problem. He had been forced to bring it down on the nearest planet for repairs. He was waiting for a repair shop to finish the work.

Andro gritted his teeth. Who was the historical character who went out in search of an honest man? He should have tried Newhouse, he thought in disgust.

The door of the bar opened, slammed shut as two txorch, their mandibles locked, rolled across the floor in front of the entrance, and then opened a crack when the arthropods had moved farther down the room. Nelsf looked in, scanned the room, and spotted Andro. He gestured for the major to come out.

"Looks like I'm wanted," Andro said, putting his glass on the floor near the wall. He reached in his pocket and pulled out a ten-crana piece. "You were right," he said, paying off his wager.

Outside he found Nelsf double-timing in place, nervous at being alone in the darkness.

"Did you find out anything?" Andro asked.

"Not about CD, something better," the mentot said, rising to stand on his four rear legs and curving his meter-long segmented body to look up at the major.

"Well?"

"Wiers has found a Halmarin. He knows where they keep the religious prisoners on Halmarin-IV."

Andro didn't believe it. The Halmarins were religious fanatics. "It has to be some sort of trap."

"I don't think so," Nelsf said, padding along by Andro's side. "He's been branded on the forehead, because he's a heretic, they said. He says he would have been burned, but he escaped and stowed away on a ship leaving the planet."

Five minutes later Andro stood facing a short, dumpy humanoid whose skin hung in folds around his face, neck, and at his wrists as if his arms were pouring out of his tunic sleeves. His eyes were glittering with avarice.

"A hundred cranas," Andro agreed. "But before I go to Halmarin-IV I'll leave word with friends. If you've lied to me, they'll be after you."

"I don't say you'll get in, or out." The Halmarin pocketed the money. "But I hope you do. If you can take a prisoner away from Charno-vins, it'll hurt him. If he could lose a few more he'd be ruined."

There wasn't any doubt about the Halmarin's sincerity. He hated the Minister of Justice. It glittered in his eyes.

Andro would have liked to find that CD, but the first priority would be to save Gella if possible. With the two mentots and the rrotta following, he headed for the old freighter. They were aboard when he noticed the rrotta's agitation.

"What's your problem, love?" he asked.

"I heard something—something I couldn't believe," Fsith said, "Onetelles is on Cornstalk."

"Cornstalk? The one in this solar system?" Nelsf's fur rippled. "There are four of us. Together we might trap him."

"We could do it." Fsith, the rrotta, extended his long legs and raised himself so he was eye to eye with Andro. "He cut off Jolpor's legs. For nothing! Because Jolpor couldn't climb a metal wall."

"He's here!" Nelsf squeaked in his agitation when Andro didn't answer. "We *have* to try."

Andro turned and headed for the cockpit. He strapped himself in while Lovey-I warmed the thrusters in preparation for take off.

Onetelles!

Onetelles down on a planet, where he didn't have to outfly him. He could take the half-breed. He might not be as fast, but in his ears he seemed to hear the millions of dead on his ancestral planet calling out for revenge.

And yet there was Gella.

He had until he reached the upper atmosphere to make up his mind about his direction.

CHAPTER 9

When Conek came out of time-comp he was still a long way from Eacher Solar System. In the early days of spaceflight he would have been weeks away from his destination. Still, he was where he wanted to be.

No shipboard computer could hold the available information on all the settled worlds in the Vladmn Territory. Conek's coordinates for the far side of Alpha Galaxy were sketchy.

The little information he had told him Orser was the second of eleven planets. He took a long-range reading, fed the information into the ship's data banks, and went back into time-comp. He didn't leave his seat. The klaxon that gave a ten-minute warning before the ship reached its destination blared as soon as the black of space grayed. The ship came back to real time and speed in three minutes. They were just above the heavy atmosphere of the second planet.

Beside him, Cge watched the sensor screens from the co-pilot's seat.

"Nobody home," the droid said, repeating a remark he had heard Conek make.

"There's someone somewhere," Conek said, hoping his information on Orser had been correct. He didn't have time to search the whole outer arm of the galaxy for a stupid outlaw planet.

Gella didn't have time.

Still the lack of evidence on civilization didn't worry him too much. A hundred years before, time-comp had changed the colonization process. The new drive, discovered on an alien ghoster, had reduced impossible distances to manageable and even practical proportions.

There were still rabbit warren worlds like Colsar, where Conek had been born, but most were sparsely settled, dependent on freighters to ship in trade goods and ship out the homegrown products. Colonization restrictions had been lowered until a thousand people could get a charter for colonization.

No freighter pilot had ever objected. It made for good business.

"Thruster emissions," Cge said, pointing to the far right-hand screen on his console just as Conek noticed them. He saw six, registering as bright orange blips. Two disappeared completely, shutting down. Another dot appeared, wavered, and steadied into a bright dot. One moved, angling to the right as it enlarged. The pattern was generally consistent with spaceports all over the three galaxies.

Conek checked to be sure his comm-link was open and started down. No one challenged him. In minutes he had come out of the cloud cover.

He frowned and shook his head as he took his first look at Orser. There were no trees, at least none within the hundreds of miles his ground sensors could reach. The ground cover was a deep, dark green, but by his computer readout, it rose no higher than five centimeters from the earth.

"A perfect place to make a forced landing," he muttered, turning toward the spaceport. The first thing he noticed was an old CD-51. Not far away was a CD-48; they were so similar the miners on Halmarin might not have known the difference.

Conek checked the charge in his blaster and replaced it in his holster. He stood for a moment considering and then returned to his stateroom. From a clothing compartment he removed a second weapon, one that would have cost more than any blaster should if Conek had purchased it. It could save his life, and cause the quinta to be asked a lot of questions if the Vladmn Space Authority discovered Conek had it.

Miniaturization of electronics had been the aim of pioneering technicians since the first practical use of electronics, but the basic blaster had not been changed since a practical power pack had been invented to fit in a hand-held weapon. The little item Conek took from his locker had a barrel the exact size of his index finger and half as thick. The grip, if it could be called one, was even shorter, designed to be activated by the press of his thumb. The deadly little weapon was permanently attached to a holster apparatus that strapped around his forearm, just above his wrist, with the weapon designed to eject from the holster and slip automatically into his hand by his flexing of his muscles.

It had been developed for planetary council members and the quinta after the rebellion. It was only a toy for them, because with their increased numbers of mentally conditioned bodyguards, they were usually too heavily surrounded to be able to get off a shot at a would-be assassin. But Conek was down on Orser. Even if he had still been in the contrabanding business, he was a stranger where suspicion was the main mechanism for survival.

"You will shoot the blaster QuintaNorden sent you?" Cge stood in the doorway watching. His vocal inflections gave him the attitude of concern.

"No, I won't be using it," Conek said, pushing up his sleeve to attach the weapon to his arm. "I'll just wear it to get the feel of it." He tried to ignore the little droid who stood in the doorway rolling back and forth within a fifteen-centimeter space. Cge's sensor panels were blinking rapidly. Conek could hear a soft hum from the unit's computer as it worked hard at some calculation.

"Humans do not have a factual restriction," Cge remarked.

Conek glowered down at his smallest droid. "Are you calling me a liar?"

"It is in Cge's data banks: ConekHayden does not wear a weapon when ConekHayden is not calculating trouble." All names, no pronouns. A certain indication the little droid was undergoing stress.

"It's always a good idea to be armed in a strange place," Conek said. He didn't add, it was also a good idea when asking questions on a world like Orser.

"Cge will accompany ConekHayden."

Conek opened his mouth to object and then closed it. Deso, the droid pilot of his Skooler vessel, had once explained to Conek how the computerized mind of a Skooler droid worked. They gave probable weights to factors based on previous experience, and Conek had no desire to ask Cge what chances the droid was giving his survival.

He didn't need to be a computer to calculate how long Cge would remain on the ship after he left it. Since Cge's remaining Skooler panels were damaged, but could still override anything the Vladmn roboticists had replaced, the droid didn't have a working restriction panel, and took orders only when they did not conflict with what he considered his higher duty, taking care of his owner.

"If I don't take you, you'll make trouble," Conek muttered, but he wasn't giving in gracefully. "But you listen to me, you rusting can of busted panels, you start any trouble and I'll use your legs to hold up a table."

"I do not rust, and I will not start any trouble," Cge said, following along behind Conek. The captain thought he heard a curious little emphasis on the word "start," but decided not to mention it. If he did, Cge would give him a logical answer and make him sound like a fool for asking.

He started for the forward hold. He had already locked the lounge elevator in place and slid a steel bar through a set of brackets he had installed. No one could use the elevator in his absence. The grav-beam on the forward hold was set to a special frequency. He wasn't taking any chances that some ship thief would get *Bucephalus*.

The landing pad was the same as on most sparsely settled worlds, unpaved but the earth had been scorched and fused by the heat of landings and takeoffs. There was a boring sameness of shape, the barren scorched donut circled a small town. It could have been any contrabanding town except for

Siddah-II and MD-439. The smugglers who took their work from Tsaral's network had the luxury of paved pads and streets.

And they were probably paid better too, Conek thought, looking at the worn, patched ships. Half the pilots on Orser were looking for fuel money, he thought.

After seeing the ships, Conek knew what to expect of the town. Some of the structures were abandoned, some lacked windows, and one was missing part of the roof. He continued until he found one that seemed reasonably sound. Over the door hung a sign that showed a flow of liquid into a glass. The timing of the light animation was broken and the result was an intermittent upward gush of light as if the liquid in the glass were exploding into the air.

"Whatever it is, I'm not drinking it," Conek said as he opened the door for Cge.

Most bars were dark inside, but this one was well lit. The reason was obvious by the odor. They were cleaning up after a brawl. Two bodies lay on the floor, both still slightly smoking after a blaster fight. One was a txorch. That wasn't unexpected; wherever there was trouble you found a txorch. The other was a Corrider, an arthropod with a vaguely human shape and a reddish exoskeleton. Their hands—they did have handlike appendages—were excellent for working with electronics. When humans reached the far side of Beta Galaxy, they found the spacefaring Corrider had settled seven star systems. Conek had never heard of them in this part of Vladmn.

"You with the droid!" the bartender yelled.

Conek looked toward the bar where a hairy talovan stood with his hands braced against the counter.

"Yes?"

"We've had enough trouble with strangers. If you're after trouble, look somewhere else."

"You're right, I can get trouble anywhere," Conek called back, forcing himself to smile. "Today I've got something else in mind."

The bartender stared at him for a moment and nodded.

"That droid can't take up a seat when the place starts filling up."

Conek doubted if the Bubbly, as the bar was named, ever had enough patrons to fill the rickety chairs, but he gave a nod of understanding and took a seat at the bar. The request was reasonable. Droids weren't paying customers since they didn't drink.

Conek ordered a Colsarian flamer, a drink he had never tasted on his home planet, since his father had taken him off Colsar when he was ten. He'd long ago decided heredity had something to do with preferred tastes and his preference for flamers was a prime example. The bartender of the Bubbly had added artificial flavor to cover the short liquor measure. Since Conek wanted his mind clear, he didn't complain. He wondered what the flavoring was. The drink was surprisingly good.

He sipped at it as he watched the few patrons under lowered lids. He was trying to decide which would be the most talkative, but it looked as if he might not have much choice. Four big talovans entered and removed the corpses, but the odor of the burned bodies hung in the air, too strong for the filters to clear immediately.

Of the ten live patrons in the bar when Conek entered, four had left by the time he finished his first drink. He ordered a second and nodded at the four-eyed jelinian two stools away.

"Makes a pretty good drink," Conek said, nodding toward the bartender.

The jelinian gave a noncommittal click and continued the search of his several pouches attached to a belt around his midsection. Conek noticed the quadraped's glass was empty.

"And another for my friend down here," Conek said when the bartender came back.

"Must've left my stash on the ship," the jelinian said, moving down a stool, but still leaving one empty between them. "Next time I'll buy. Name's Wigger."

"Sure," Conek said, trying to make it sound as if he believed Wigger. He'd been around enough bars to recognize the ploy, but the local moocher would be more likely to talk than many of the others. He introduced himself and gave his real name. With *Bucephalus* sitting on the landing pad, there was no point in using an alias. He was right. Wigger gave him a four-eyed once-over.

"Heard about you. Got them big Osalt ships. Ship for Tsaral sometimes."

"Right, but not much anymore. They're big enough to make the legal stuff profitable, but now that I'm right-side running, they are a problem at times. Too big for some small, short hauls."

"Don't see why you want to make small, short hauls," the bartender said as he put the jelinian's drink down in front of him.

"I don't want to, but most clients with the big money hauls have some headache work they want to unload in the contract. I either take it or lose out. I'm looking for something in the CD class. Know of any for sale?"

"Funny, you're the second one to ask that in two days," the talovan said. "How come CDs are in demand all of a sudden?"

"I don't know and I don't like hearing it," Conek said, and meant it. He wondered if one of Skielth's friends had made planet-fall here. "I decided on that type of small freighter because they're cheap and not too hard to repair. If the price goes up, I'll switch my choice, I guess."

He gave a sigh. "But I did want a couple. Know of any around?"

"Don't know of any that might be for sale," Wigger said, finishing off his drink and pushing the empty glass suggestively toward the bartender.

"Know of any pilots with CDs?" Conek asked, nodding to the talovan to refill Wigger's glass.

"Funny, but that's the same thing the other one asked," the bartender said. "Don't know that we can help you." He reached out a large hairy hand and scooped Conek's second drink off the counter along with Wigger's empty glass.

Well, no doubt about it, Conek had worn out his welcome in the Bubbly. He'd have to look elsewhere for his information. And if Skielth or one of the Shashar had already checked Orser, then he was already pumping a dry well.

He pulled out a crana piece and held it out, but the bartender ignored it. Conek pocketed the money and left the bar, heading back for his ship. Cge rolled at his side.

"There are no CDs for sale here," Cge said, summing up the conversation for his data banks.

"None for sale, but one isn't far off," Conek said. "The talovan either knows about the one I'm after, or one in some rough trade. He's scared, and it takes a lot to shake those lion-maned devils."

"He did not appear to be frightened," Cge said dubiously.

"When he wouldn't take the money for a drink, he was letting someone know he wasn't selling information. Someone in that bar." Conek thought back, trying to remember the six customers that had remained. The jelinian. Two humans had been sitting at a table in the rear of the bar. They had seemed too intent on a holo game to notice anyone else was there, but they could have been good actors. Two xrotha and a Olynthr had been sitting at a table closer to the front. It would have been easy for them to overhear the conversation.

"I'd put my money on the xrotha," Conek muttered, his decision based on nothing more than his dislike of the six-legged crablike creatures. He looked over his shoulder. He'd been followed in broad daylight before. No one seemed to be following him, but unless he walked backward all the way to the ship, he couldn't be sure.

He was checking his back trail again when a beam from a blaster sailed by him and browned a spot on the side of the building immediately to his left. His reflexes threw him into a sprint for the two paces it took to reach the corner of the building.

His blaster was in his hand by the time he skidded around the corner and pressed himself against the wall. He stood listening, he could hear hurried footsteps. He looked around the corner, his weapon ready.

A female rrotta was hurrying down the street, a bundle of

purchases on the top of her flat carapace. In between her long legs, five young rrotta scampered along, staying beneath her wide shell. When she saw the blaster in Conek's hand she gave a series of frightened clicks. Since she wasn't wearing a translator, he couldn't understand her, but it wasn't hard to figure out she wanted to get her brood out of danger.

Conek's appearance was enough for his ambusher, and another beam made another scorch on the building, narrowly missing both Conek and the rrotta.

The next shelter large enough to hold both her and her brood was half a block up the street. The female looked about, made her decision, and dashed into the alley behind Conek.

"Of all the flaming—" Conek muttered. That's what being kind to Mama and the kids got him. Now he'd have to leave or risk getting them shot if his ambushers moved in on him. And while he was thinking of little ones, where was Cge?

He pressed himself to the side of the building again and shouted.

"Cge!"

No answer.

"Cge!"

Still nothing.

Well, the little character could take care of himself in a pinch. At least he knew to turn his back on anyone with a blaster. His body metal was impervious to a killing beam. Only his sensor panels were vulnerable.

Conek risked another quick look and saw the edge of a talovan mane and the end of a blaster appear around the edge of a building across the street and up about ten meters. He dropped a shot just over the talovan's head and the big humanoid ducked back again. Conek moved out of sight, took another quick look, and ducked again. As far as he could tell there was only one ambusher.

Still, one was enough.

There should be some way he could get around one, though. He looked down the alley wondering if there was a way out. It appeared to be a dead end, but it couldn't be. Mama and the kids had disappeared. Then he saw the moving dirt. She had dug a hole for the brood and as he watched she was pushing dirt out of a second hole. He could just barely see the bundles still on her back.

Smart lady, he thought, but the fact that she had not looked for an exit told him there wasn't one that way. The only way out was the street.

He was taking a couple of deep breaths and getting set to make a run for it when he heard the talovan start to shout. From across the street he heard the hiss of blaster fire, but the weapon had not stopped whatever was bothering Conek's attacker.

Conek looked out to see the talovan come into view, pushed by a large packing crate. The crate bumped and shoved at the maned humanoid, keeping him slightly off balance. While the talovan fought with the square plasteel crate, he had no time to shoot. Beneath the upturned carton, Conek could see a pair of gray cupped droid feet, the extended wheels zipping back and forth.

Conek stepped out in the street and leveled his weapon.

"Drop it," he ordered the talovan.

The humanoid tried aiming at Conek, got bumped by the carton, and gave up. He threw down the blaster.

"That's enough, little buddy," Conek said and watched half amused as after struggling to lift the crate off himself, Cge gave up and turned it on its side, going down with it. He reappeared, crawling out of the box, and stood up, scanning his owner.

"ConekHayden functions correctly?"

"Right on specification," Conek replied and then turned to stare at his ambusher. "What did I do to you?"

"We don't like strangers asking questions."

"Why, if you don't have anything to hide?"

"It's none of your business what we use our ships for," the talovan growled. "You got no authority on this planet."

This conversation was taking a strange turn.

"I haven't got any *authority* anywhere," Conek said. "I came looking for some ships. I don't care what you're into —that's not true—I think I want to know."

"And you can just keep wanting." The talovan didn't seem to want to cooperate, so Conek raised his blaster and fired at the wall behind the big maned humanoid. He ignored the first shot. He turned his eyes at the second. It was close enough to singe his mane. As Conek started lining up for the third, the talovan moved his head.

"My information won't do you any good. I just pick the stuff up. I don't know who the contacts on Niltea are."

"Niltea?" Conek stared at the talovan. "What the hell has Niltea got to do with it?"

It was the talovan's time to look confused. "What did you think we did with the hermil—*eat* it?"

"Hermil!" Conek swore long and hard. Hermil was a synthetic fiber made from a plant on one of the planets in the arm. He didn't remember which. Ten years before there had been some uproar about the famous Niltean carpets being made with hermil. Niltea made a territory-wide announcement that they were banning shipments of the synthetic from the planet. Obviously not all the carpet weavers agreed with the ban, since the supply of the famous Niltean wool was not keeping up with the demand for the rugs. Why hadn't he thought about that market when he was still contrabanding?

Knowing he had missed a lucrative opportunity made him nearly as angry as being ambushed, and added to that, the smuggler he had flushed wasn't the one he wanted.

"Of all the stupid—" he ran out of words for a moment. He took a deep breath and thought up some more. "I ought to stuff your whole damn cargo down your throat. What the hell do I want with it? I've got other things on my mind."

"You're not working with the Vladmn Patrol?" the talovan asked, sounding as confused as Conek felt.

Conek denied it, yelling a little more just to let off steam. Then he remembered there were two CDs on the donut.

"The fifty-one is mine," the talovan admitted, looking sheepish after being convinced Conek wasn't after him.

"And the forty-eight? Remember, you owe me after that stunt."

"Don't think the forty-eight's for sale." The talovan scratched his mane thoughtfully. "Belongs to a couple of cynbeth. They bought it grounded for repairs about six years ago. Been flying for—for others and working on it in their spare time as they got parts. Only had it flying again about a year."

Conek swore again.

"Know of any more around?"

"I don't," the smuggler said. "I don't stray much from here except when I'm shipping. I help my brother in the Bubbly."

So that's why the bartender threw him out.

Conek gave a sigh and hoped the others were having better luck than he was.

"Come on, Cge," he ordered and started for *Bucephalus*.

He hoped he would have better luck on Siddah-II. If he didn't, Gella might not get off Halmarin-IV.

CHAPTER 10

Skielth stood beside a pile of discarded parts that appeared to be the leftovers from a destruction team gone berserk. He watched a grease-covered Mitiskik shove the bare ends of several wires into some jury-rigged clips and stand back to admire his work. It was a sloppy job.

"That'll keep him going for a while," the big arthropod thruster technician said as he leaned against what appeared to be the oldest ship's engine in Vladmn.

"Yeah," Skielth said, and kept his thoughts to himself. He wouldn't have lifted a ship with that thruster if he could have picked it up with two hands.

The FarArm of Alpha Galaxy had always been called the junkyard of space, and he could see why. It wasn't just the age of the vessels; if this grease ant was an example of the technical quality, the maintenance the ships received was little better than nothing. Always on the lookout for a money-making opportunity, he thought a good ships' repair shop on one of the neighboring planets would probably make a fortune and put this sloppy character out of business.

He didn't say so. The Mitiskik had been the first one on the planet to give him any information.

"Don't think you could be looking for Inchis, though,"

the sticklike insect told him, turning his long head to stare out the door of the dilapidated hangar. His mandibles quivered as he saw a smaller flying creature flutter from a corner of the hangar into the light. With a bound he was after it. His two-meter-long tongue flashed out. He came back to Skielth, chewing his catch.

"He never gets over to the Beta side."

"This fellow said he didn't very often," Skielth pursued. "I sure would like to find him." He had repeated his cover story until he was almost ready to believe it himself. "Wish I hadn't been too drunk to remember the particulars. I just remember he was swearing at his CD-51 and he mentioned half a dozen planets in the conversation. I was too hazy to catch which one he took his downtime on. He said he needed a good ship and pilot and there was plenty of money in the work."

The arthropod gave a series of clicks that translated into a laugh.

"If there's money in something, it ain't here," he said. "I came here thinking a good repair shop would bring it in. Even them that has a few cranas welsh on their debts. There's nothing for nobody on this side of Alpha unless you're into trade that don't get mentioned."

"And who's into that?" Skielth asked, trying to make his voice sly.

The Mitiskik had been friendly up until that time, but he drew back, reaching for a retractor bar. At first Skielth thought the insect meant to attack, but he turned away and slipped the clip end into another thruster.

"Don't know and don't want to know," the Mitiskik said. "I fix ships, I don't ask the pilots what they do with them. That could get me a blaster bolt in the worst possible spot."

"Never been into that trade myself," Skielth replied hastily, hoping to keep the technician talking.

"Didn't ask and don't want to know. I got to get this thruster ready by nightfall."

The conversation was over. Skielth thanked the Mitiskik and ambled out of the hangar. He walked as if he were enjoying the sporadic sunshine, but he was wishing he could shake some information out of the residents. Center was a planet that had been mined out and abandoned by the Amal when it first came into power. Space drifters had moved in and settled on it, eking out a living in agriculture and raising flocks of ratty-looking ovines.

They were a motley, suspicious crew, and watched him as if he were after their last bite of wilweed, a bitter, wide-leafed plant they boiled and seemed to relish, though the stench nauseated him.

He wasn't going to learn any more there, he decided, and turned toward the landing area where he had left his ship. He had nearly reached it when he heard a footstep behind him and turned in time to see a human slipping behind the leg of a rusty Hidderan winger.

The winger was an awkward ship, made up of large pipes and balls, and the thickest part of it was its landing legs, all eight of them. They were thick enough to hide the bulk of a Shashar, and Skielth took advantage of one. He did a rapid, silent backtrack to the leg nearest him and stepped into its shadow, keeping it between himself and his pursuer.

He waited for more than a minute before peering around the side of the support. Two legs away, a scruffy-looking human was in full sight with his back to Skielth. He stood with his blaster in his right hand, his left was scratching his head. He peered farther around the leg, looking in the general direction Skielth would have been walking if he hadn't caught sight of his ambusher.

"So you want to find me, little man," the Shashar murmured. In spite of their bellowing voices, Shashar could be quiet when they chose.

"I'd hate to think I disappointed you."

He moved forward with reptilian stealth, going first to the shelter of another, closer leg. He could see the human watching the direction the Shashar would have been going if he had continued toward his ship. Skielth had to reach the man before he realized he had stopped being the hunter and was now the hunted. It would be easy for him to slip around the leg, using it for cover and have Skielth out in the open.

Since Skielth hadn't made a sound, it must have been the

man's natural wariness that alerted him to his danger. He turned, let out a gasp, and lunged around the support leg, but he wasn't fast enough to evade the big reptile.

Skielth closed on him in two bounds, and caught the human by the neck, his rapier-tipped claws threatening to slice into the man's windpipe.

"Let—let me go, I didn't do anything," the man pleaded. His bloodshot eyes were pleading, dripping tears. His whining disgusted the Shashar who thought about taking his weapon and throwing the crud to the ground.

But the man's attempted ambush was an answer to the questions he had been asking. All he had to do was find out what that answer meant.

If he learned anything, he wouldn't be able to use it if the man had friends hiding somewhere on the field.

"Move," Skielth ordered, yanking the character along. The man had trouble keeping up with the Shashar's grip on his neck.

"I didn't do anything," the man gasped, half strangled.

"You're going to. You're going to tell me all about why you were so interested in me."

CHAPTER 11

Lagon Fellerd stood facing Ulcher, but this time they were physically together. They needed direct communication; no codes would answer Fellerd's questions, and their problem wasn't a subject that could be discussed on a public access transmission.

The helovan was still terrified. He no longer worried about the result of not locating the lost shipment. He was half a galaxy away. At that moment he was bothered by the threat of his cleosar employer. Fellerd just might tear his head off.

He tried to think, to find a way to divert the cleosar's anger from himself, but he had searched and worked, ignoring his body's need to be soaked until his skin was cracked and stinging and the inside of his gills felt like they had been filled with sand. The webbing between his fingers itched, but if he scratched it he could tear the skin.

He didn't worry overmuch about the cleosar's threatening crouch. He was more concerned with his superior's eye stalks. Normally they rose thirty centimeters or more above their body shells, but in times of suspicion or possible danger, the stalks shrunk to a quarter their usual length. Fellerd's were down close to his body.

"Who could know those fanatics on Halmarin-IV would

be after the pilot of that CD?'' Ulcher pointed out, even though he could not be blamed for the shipment that had gone astray. That part of the job was in Fellerd's hands. Still, if he could placate the cleosar, his own neck might be safer.

He took a deep breath and tried to keep his gill flaps from fluttering. They calmed a bit as Fellerd's eye stalks lengthened. Two of the cleosar's visual orbs turned away from him and faced each other, a typical habit of the species when considering an issue. The action gave the impression the eyes were consulting as if they were two separate entities.

Fellerd was listening. He decided to press his advantage.

"Who could have known they'd want to punish her for something her father did?"

"No one knew!" Fellerd exploded. "No one knew about her, about them, or about us! Now everyone knows about her, her father, the Halmarins, and the missing ship! And when they find it they'll know more! More than we can afford! Why are they putting so much effort into finding one old, decrepit ship anyway?"

Ulcher knew the answer, but he shrugged his thick, scaled shoulders. He didn't think it the proper time to tell Fellerd about the CD that had landed on a Halmarin planet for repairs and had burned some locals who came to investigate. It also wasn't the best time to mention they had been using legal registration numbers from ships that flew exclusively in the Holton/Beta side of Alpha Galaxy.

It was just bad luck that they had let some of the locals escape after they had time to read the registration number. It was worse luck that Fellerd had sent a shipment on a freighter that carried that same number.

The chances of it happening were too astronomical to figure, and if he could handle the mathematics, he wouldn't know how to read that many decimal points.

But it had happened.

"Maybe they were shipping something *they* didn't want found." Ulcher made an effort to shift the blame from himself and his people, though he had not been responsible for choosing a hauler that endangered the shipment. He was too shrewd to point that out to the cleosar.

Fellerd paused thoughtfully. Then his eye stalks bobbed.

"Could be. No way to run a legitimate business, though." He sounded insulted, as if Hayden Haulers had created a breach of business ethics in carrying contraband, endangering Fellerd's illegal shipments.

Ulcher let the irony slip by. This was no time to anger his superior.

"How could that fool Chukin—" Fellerd sputtered and paused. He didn't have the right words. He could not understand the stupidity of his simian area lieutenant who had sent an io-head, a doper, to keep an eye on one of Hayden's Shashar cronies who had been asking too many questions.

The io-head had been caught, and if he knew anything, he'd talk his head off for a fix.

"The crawler—" Fellerd used the term the organization had coined for the io-heads who would do anything for a dose. "Where was he from? Could he know anything?"

Ulcher's protruding eyes shifted before he controlled them to look the cleosar directly in his wavering stalks.

"Chukin was on comm-link." He didn't need to say more. Fellerd would know Ulcher had received only a minimum of information. Luckily he had been off Vilarona when the ape had had his bright idea.

"We have to do something," Ulcher said. "I got out most of my people, but we won't be able to move the equipment until the magnetic storm's over."

"By that time it will be too late," Fellerd said. "It's time to call in the heavy weapons."

Ulcher looked confused, and Fellerd didn't enlighten him. He sent the helovan back to his work.

As he watched Ulcher walk away he dug his clawed hands into the dirt of the open ground, needing physical force in his frustration. He had expected to take his anger out on the helovan, but the amphibian's panic a few days before had calmed since he wasn't being blamed for the loss of the shipment.

And he had been working to find it, that was clear by the cracked skin on his neck and cheeks. He had been going without his daily four-hour soaks his species usually required.

But Ulcher hadn't found that ship. Maybe no one would. Matters had gone beyond his ability to handle. He would have to report to his boss, the head of the organization.

He hoped he could report and make it back alive.

Onetelles didn't like bad news, and he had a big appetite.

CHAPTER 12

"I'm going to tiptoe in and out and play the big hero," Andro muttered as he strapped himself in the pilot's seat on the old CC-12. The alarm had sounded, indicating they were coming out of time-comp.

"I am not programmed to tiptoe," Lovey-I answered as he scanned the instruments from the copilot's seat.

"Neither is this rumbling old rattletrap," Andro muttered. Nobody sneaked onto a planet, not a colonized one with their own atmospheric space authority, anyway.

As he waited for the time-comp to bring them back to normal space, he decided he must have been insane to even think of going to Halmarin-IV.

He had listened to a Halmarin heretic, Doochin, who had insisted he could fly on and off the planet without being spotted. It was impossible, but at the time he was fired by the ambition to be a knight in sterling armor, or whatever those pre-space primitives called themselves.

Dearie, you've been around these macho-type heroes far too long. But now was a fine time to tell himself that.

"Set an alternate comp program so we can get out in a hurry when we're spotted," he told Lovey-I. He couldn't pretend to hope any longer. When he saw the slowed responses, he added, "I don't care where, back toward Newhouse, and far enough away so we won't be shot at."

Then he decided to set it himself. Making the decision was something that would keep him busy and if he needed to use the coordinates he would know where he was going.

At least he had retained that much sanity.

Then the gray of time-comp gave way to—brown?

And all his instruments went crazy at once.

"My sensor's malfunctioning," Lovey-I said, his voice wavering.

"Shut down!" Andro ordered. "Shut down now!" Conek would strangle him if anything happened to Lovey-I who had become indispensable with his talent for looking after his owner's creature comforts. The major cursed himself for not considering the droid's sensors, but he had not really believed they would find Halmarin in the midst of a magnetic storm.

"If the rest of his information is correct, we just might do it," he muttered as he struggled to manually pilot the ship.

It was common knowledge that once every three years Griffin, a systemless star in Janus sector, gave out with a solar hiccup. She had been at it for a couple of hundred years, but less than twenty years before, it was discovered that something she emitted had reached some of the stars in Alpha Galaxy's FarArm. As a result they threw periodic fits corresponding with Griffin's time cycle. The solar scientists were too busy steepling their fingers and tutting over the layman's inability to understand the problem to figure it out.

Andro hadn't really believed the branded heretic. He gave the wrinkled little runt a mental apology.

But could he land the unwieldy CC-12 without the use of his computer? Without the computer to balance the power output, the drag of one raggedly running portside thruster was attempting to pull him off course. Without the computers to run the hydros, he was having to strain at the controls. He dipped into the atmosphere, timed his descent, and aimed roughly for the south pole of the planet until he was low enough to catch a glimpse of the sea. It, at least, wasn't brown in the middle, but looked rusty around the edges.

The sky was gray-brown, tinged with dawn. The plan was

for him to arrive just as the sun was rising, but if he had miscalculated, he could miss his first landmark in the dark. Had he missed it? He thought he had descended a long way before it was light enough to make out deviations in the coastline. Once he descended out of the upper atmosphere, he had been warned to keep to a low altitude.

But he couldn't hang around and wait. Every year Halmarin was plagued with violent windstorms and huge thick dust clouds, and according to Doochin, this year they were due to hit at the same time as the magnetic storm. They rounded the planet with the daylight, and if Andro found himself in one without his sensors, trying to find the ground would be suicide.

The light was still hazy when he saw the landmark Doochin had given him, a two-pronged promontory of jutting land. From there he was to angle east and set his course to take him low over the saddle between two mountain cliffs.

He suffered a few uneasy minutes before he saw the mountains. They were as bleak and barren as Doochin had promised. And just as he had promised, on the other side of the range was a small, abandoned spaceport.

Andro brought the old CC-12 down to a thousand meters and angled slightly to the right, allowing for the yaw caused by the uneven thruster power in the old vessel.

My dear, you could be Alpha FarArm smuggler, he congratulated himself as the ship settled into its flight path.

"The port is exactly where Doochin said it would be," he called out, loud enough to be heard in the compartment behind the cockpit. He had momentarily forgotten that the rrotta and the two mentots aboard were blaming him for not going after Onetelles.

They had also doubted the Halmarin. They were willing to help rescue Gella, and weren't afraid of going into a hostile city, but if there was a chance they might not make it back from Halmarin, they wanted a shot at the half-breed butcher before they went.

When he insisted on trying for Gella first, they were passive in their disapproval, not insisting, but the spark had gone out of them. He had explained the urgency of getting Gella off Halmarin-IV, and added he had promised Conek Hayden not to risk his droid by chasing Onetelles with Lovey-I aboard the ship. He had pointed out that they were trusting him to keep his word to them, but could they trust it if he didn't keep faith with Captain Hayden?

Very weak, dearie, they don't see Conek's protectiveness of his droids in the same light as their need for revenge, he told himself.

When the CC-12 settled to the surface of fused earth, he left the thrusters idling and unstrapped himself.

Back in the living compartment the rrotta was roped against a bulkhead cushioned with resilient cargo buffer material. The two mentots were strapped in the loungers.

"Surprise, sweethearts, we made it," Andro said as he walked over to the food dispenser and punched up a carton of revitalizing fluid. He took a sip.

"I had the escape coordinates programmed in, but Doochin's instructions were accurate."

"Then you think he told us the truth." Nelsf unstrapped himself and crept down off the lounger, two sets of feet at a time. His thin fur still rippled with doubt.

"About the port, at least." Wiers, who had found the Halmarin, had become their strongest disbeliever. He was working on a good case of preguilt pangs, afraid his discovery of the heretic would get himself and all his friends killed. He had worked hard to talk them out of it.

"Correct, dearie, so make up your minds. Are you going with me or not?"

Andro was willing to give them a few minutes to think it over, but they didn't take the time.

"We are," Fsith announced while he freed himself from the last knots of his makeshift safety harness. "Onetelles may be gone from Cornstalk before we get back there. When he hears we got the pilot out . . ."

Fsith left the others to think of the half-breed's anger while he struggled with the last knot and picked up his breather mask. According to their information, the rrotta and the mentots were immune to the effects of clin-gas, but they would still be bothered by the dust.

"Then it's time to move—on with our dash and do!" Andro gave a little dance step as he finished off the last of his revitalized drink and put on his own mask. To his amusement the mentots solemnly imitated him as well as they could with their four stubby rear legs. Their segmented bodies rippled with the motion.

The morning wind was already raising dust clouds when they left the ship. Andro went to the nearest hangar that looked as if it were sturdy enough to stand for another day and enlisted the aid of the mentots to help him open the doors. He sent the rrotta down to the third building to look for Doochin's hopper.

According to the escaped Halmarin, he had hidden it under some loose wall panels and rotting electric cables. If it was still there and usable, Fsith would have the best chance of finding it in the darkness.

Andro had taxied the ship into the hangar, the mentots had loaded their packs with food parcels, and they were closing the hangar when Fsith came back.

He had uncovered the vehicle, its power supply had lasted, and it appeared to be in running condition. He hurried off to help Nelsf and Wiers close one of the hangar doors and Andro wondered what the rrotta had not wanted to tell him.

He wasn't long in finding out what he should have known. The battered little hopper was meant to transport Halmarins, and only Halmarins.

"This is going to be a mess," Andro said as he drove the little vehicle out into the open. His knees were jacked up to his chin and splayed, since he had to reach between them to get at the controls.

The mentots were able to use the seats, but only by climbing in so they faced backward. To face the front they corkscrewed their segmented bodies until they had legs sticking out in all directions.

Fsith didn't fit at all. He had to be tied onto the small cargo platform on the back. He eyed the slick surface and clicked to himself until Andro restarted the engine and muffled his worries.

Their directions called for them to travel down an unused road for nearly an hour before they came to their first landmark and took off across country.

"There." Nelsf pointed to a rock formation. "That must be it, but the face must be on the other side."

Andro passed the three tall rocks and slowed. He heard the scrape of exoskeleton against metal and heard Fsith's worried clicking. Every time they changed speed, direction, or hit a bump the rrotta knew he was falling off.

"It has a face," Wiers said, looking back and up at the wind-scarred rock. His translator sounded his relief. The instructions were perfect. The Halmarin had told them they needed to be detailed because they would have limited vision. He had been right.

But Andro was worried. The directions seemed to him to be too perfect. Either the Halmarin had nearly perfect recall, or someone had taken a lot of trouble to make sure the rescuers didn't get lost.

They were more than four hours on the circuitous path out of the mountains before they approached the outskirts of the small capital city. A direct path would have taken them into the eastern quarter, but Doochin had insisted they should approach and leave from the southwestern section.

All the streets in the area connected with the road to the main spaceport and a smaller landing field a little distance to the north. If they were discovered and followed, the Halmarins would assume they were aiming for one of those two ports.

Also, most of the businesses in the area were warehouses for off-world trade, and since few pilots would risk flying in magnetic storms, the area would probably be deserted.

"You won't have any trouble when you get to the city, because everyone stays inside during the dust storms," Doochin had said.

"He would pick this one time to be wrong," Andro said

as they passed the second warehouse and heard voices, shouting in anger and alarm.

He decided he had better find a place to hide, but he wasn't quite quick enough in making the decision. Just as he turned into an alley, a block away a speeder came around the corner and straight at them.

CHAPTER 13

Conek heard the Agnar-Alphan port controller screaming because he had comped too close to the flight lanes on his reentry from space.

"So complain to Quinta Norden," he snarled.

"The quinta do not manage the spaceports," Cge informed him, showing off his limited political knowledge.

"Why not? She tries to run everything else," he griped. "How are we supposed to find out who burned those miners if she keeps sticking her nose in?"

The droid didn't answer, and if he had, Conek would have ignored him. He demanded clearance to land in a voice that made it plain one flight controller had better not set foot outside the tower if he denied it.

Conek had his priority clearance and was dropping in over his hangar when he saw the small ground zipper just inside the already opened doors.

Perversity and a desire not to waste time made him decide not to enter the hangar. The moment he shut his thrusters down the zipper scooted out in the sunlight for the forty seconds it took for it to reach the shade of the ship's left wing. As it raced across the pavement, Conek could see the handsome Lieutenant Marwit at the controls and Quinta Norden sitting by him.

Judging by the ground vehicle's neck-breaking speed-up and its sudden halt by the spot where the lounge lift would descend, the quinta wasn't interested in wasting time either.

Conek used the controls in the cockpit to lower the passenger elevator. He hurriedly unstrapped his safety harness and rushed to the lounge to meet his visitor. He might be angry with Norden for calling him back from his search, but she was still a quinta.

When the lifter rose and joined with the lounge floor again, Norden was alone. She was carrying a Vladmn Patrol coded information disk and part of a decoder. She came hurrying across the floor, a little skip in her step as if she were still in her teens.

"Now tell me you don't have a VladPat code breaker."

"That depends on when they last changed the code," Conek replied, unwilling to give her the satisfaction of hearing a denial.

"If you do, we won't waste time hooking this one in to your computer," she said, dodging around him to reach the cockpit.

"What VladPat information am I to be privileged to see?"

"Just the incidental unregistered flight sightings in the Alpha FarArm," Norden snapped. "I can't get out there myself, but I *can* bring information in."

"I'm impressed." Conek meant it. His anger faded away. His lack of success caused him to doubt she had found much of value, but she had put out an effort to help Gella. He ordered Cge out of the copilot's seat and took it himself, allowing Norden the command seat. She had flown Osalt freighters before and had taken *Bucephalus* into battle against the Amal a year before.

She had also known about the information longer than he had and had probably made some plan for searching it. No matter how mad she made him, he never made the mistake of forgetting her intelligence.

"There's a lot here," Norden said. "Let's see what happens if we ask for the information only on CD-51s." She glanced up and saw the doubt on his face. "I *know* it could have been a similar model, but we have to start somewhere. Unregistered flights flying on and off Halmarin-IV?"

"As good as any to begin with," Conek replied, though he thought it would be a waste of time. Those fanatically religious runts were half crazy, but he didn't suspect them of being dishonest. The way Charno-vins had refused the bribe, slightly insulted, but overlooking it for form's sake, Conek thought he'd go a long way before he offered a bribe to another Halmarin.

And he'd been right in his doubts. The computer decoded the information, sorted it, scanned it, and came up with a blank.

"The miners that survived said they had thought the ship had made an emergency landing," Conek reminded Norden. "That may have been its one and only time on Halmarin-IV."

"They certainly aren't making a habit of unregistered flights." She sighed and ran a hand through her perfectly arranged hair, dislodging a few strands.

Two hours later she had completely destroyed her hairdo. Just looking at the mass of information was enough to keep them hopeful, but they had not pinpointed anything useful. The Alpha Galaxy area called the FarArm was littered with old CDs. It seemed to be where the old ships went to die.

They were still bent over the consoles when the close-in warning beeper sounded, indicating thruster activity within collision range. Conek looked up to see Skielth's Shashar Streamer coming down close by. Norden also recognized the ship.

"He wouldn't be on Agnar-Alpha if he didn't have something that couldn't wait," Conek told her.

The quinta knew Skielth was a smuggler, but he did have some legal trade. He needed it to keep a legal registration and a license. The spaceport controllers had no reason to stop him. Norden gave a resigned sigh and agreed to be deaf to anything she heard that she shouldn't

While they watched from the cockpit, Skielth lowered the cargo ramp on the low-slung ship. He rode it down as he strode out, jerking a skinny, ragged human along with him. With a speed that threatened to pull the human off his feet, the big reptile covered the distance between the two ships. Conek reached across Norden and lowered the lounge lift.

Conek went to greet his friend, wanting to break it to him that what he said would be overheard by Norden.

He didn't get a chance.

The second Skielth's head came in sight he started bellowing.

"It's iocineil, Hayden, and Gella was shipping it!"

Before Conek could speak, Norden stepped into the lounge, her black eyes snapping.

"You've been using the company Andro and I *vouched* for to smuggle additives, Captain Hayden?"

CHAPTER 14

When Sis-Silsis agreed to leave rescue of Gella Icor and his eldest slither in the hands of Conek and the pilots who flew for him, he had lied. He had pretended to agree because to continue to argue would have kept them on Agnar-Alpha trying to convince him. If he had not seemed convinced, Major Avvin might have found a way to ground him. He had never trusted his employer's friendship with a major in the Vladmn Patrol.

Sis-Silsis hated lying to Conek Hayden. It was against the cynbeth code to lie to a friend. Most species with their thousands of rules, laws, and ethics abided by them when it was convenient and ignored them when they were in the way. The cynbeth recognized few laws, but they kept them with a nearly religious fervor.

Lying to his friends had been hard for Sis-Silsis, but they didn't understand the importance of Risee. Before the plague on Cargonasse the cynbeth population had been a little over two billion. Less than five thousand had survived and most of the males were impotent. Even with Vladmn's help and all their resources, their species was dangerously close to extinction. Another plague could destroy the rest of their people.

In an effort to prevent a complete annihilation, Vladmn had ceded the planet of Farrat in Beta sector to the cynbeth for colonization, but the females who had been transported there were not laying as many eggs.

He knew Conek and the others put a high value on Gella Icor's life, and so did he, but they were not cynbeth and could never understand how important Risee could be to his entire species.

One of the main concerns of the Vladmn Space Council was to oversee the protection of the species, and to Sis-Silsis they were a danger as great as the Halmarins. Some idiot was sure to pressure the Halmarins into returning Gella and Risee, on the grounds that Risee was important to his species's survival.

According to the Halmarin faith, it was their duty to stamp out reptiles as being something conjured up by the Gervain, the creator of all evil. They would see it as their duty to destroy Risee because of his importance.

Sis-Silsis knew he could not land on Halmarin-IV and storm the prison—he supposed Gella and Risee were being kept in some sort of jail—but cynbeth were the Vladmn masters at breaking codes, and if he could pick up one to break, he could monitor their transmissions for anything that might be helpful.

First he had to drop off the shipment Conek had given him. He itched with irritation at not being able to go straight to the Halmarin system, but delivering the shipment was important, not only to keep at least part of his word to Conek, but *Destria* had been loaded with medical supplies, mainly kirbonil, which had an extremely short shelf life. For his own safety and the safety of the slithers he had on board, he needed to lighten the ship in case he had to maneuver in a hurry.

He had delivered the shipment to Hinkson in Beta Galaxy, and had punched in the coordinates to bring him back into normal space in Chirras sector. He knew Deso was due to rise after picking up a load of fiber used in food production on Agnar-Alpha where the crops were often destroyed by asteroid storms.

"Colsar port is too crowded to land now," he muttered

the emergency code as he sent the same sentence out in a sector-wide blast of communication that should reach the huge Skooler ship, but would not go far beyond it.

Moments later he received a transmission burst.

"Will rise and join you, three hours," Deso had replied. The originator code said the originator was Madder Drumps, pilot.

Though Deso had been activated and designed to be the emergency pilot of the Skooler vessel, in Vladmn no droid could be given a pilot's license, so the registered pilot was Madder Drumps. How Madder had managed a pilot's license was a mystery to everyone who knew him. He was a scientist, a specialist in atmospheres and their effects on every species from the Aablonians to Wuttshims. In return for signing on as the pilot of *Windsong*, Conek had allowed him to bring his laboratory aboard the ship. His quarters and his working area took up three staterooms, a relatively small area.

For Madder it was a dream come true. When they weren't pushed to carry cargo, Deso took the ship into the atmospheres of uninhabited planets to gather samples for the scientist. Madder left the flying of the ship entirely in the hands of the big droid who followed Conek's orders with the slavish obedience of a mechanical.

But if Sis-Silsis was to complete his plan, Deso would have to be sidetracked from that obedience. He unstrapped the safety webbing in the pilot's seat and looked across at Hercules, the Skooler worker droid that also belonged to Conek Hayden and was now programmed as his emergency pilot.

"No use in sitting here," he said to the droid, who looked up from the screens he was monitoring. Since he had not given Hercules an order, the droid turned back to the screens. He was amenable to any command Sis-Silsis gave him, but left to himself he would remain in the copilot's seat day after day without moving.

Sis-Silsis left him there and went back into the lounge. The floor and the upholstered seats glittered with little gold cynbeth. Some had hatched late, and had not developed their legs. Some were showing limbs but had not yet learned to use them. They moved around on the floor, pushing themselves along with their short coils like snakes. Others were just learning to walk, while some were walking well. Some were climbing up on the loungers and making experimental flights. The oldest had developed their ability to fly and were soaring and dipping about the room. Their parent unceremoniously pushed the creepers and crawlers out of his path with his feet, but he automatically located and identified each of his three hundred and twenty-six offspring within seconds. He hurried across the room to where one of the oldest was crouched on the back of a lounger, his body hunched as if he were in pain.

He looked closely and found a small dull spot on Gisar's wing where he had bumped into the wall and bruised himself. The injury was nothing much, he knew Gisar was putting on an act to get sympathy, but Gisar and Risee had been close companions, and the green-gold missed his red-gold companion. He let the injured slither climb up on his back.

"Sis find Risee," he said hopefully.

"We'll try," Sis-Silsis answered, checking the rest of his brood, making sure they had adequate food in their feeders and getting himself some nourishment while he waited for Deso to raise *Windsong* and join him.

He was able to finish his chores and catch an hour's sleep before Hercules signaled him to come to the cockpit. Gisar was still moaning about his bruised wingtip, so Sis-Silsis was still carrying him on his back. When he arrived the view screen shields were down and he could just see the huge black ship in front and off to port.

He didn't waste time before explaining to Deso what he wanted.

"It is not possible," Deso answered immediately. "I cannot stay undetected off Halmarin-IV and monitor the commwaves as I did at Agnar-Alpha."

"Eat him up," Gisar suggested. In the wild, a cynbeth hatching brought Annikes, predatory birds, and since the hatchlings were as hungry as their hunters, three or more often brought down a bird and ate it. It was the instinct of the slithers to eat anything they saw as unfriendly.

"Why can't you?" Sis-Silsis demanded, ignoring his

slither. His frustration was making him angry. It crossed his mind that the robot was refusing to put himself out for two sentients. He had hung in space long enough when he wanted to find another robot.

"At that time I was alone. With PilotDrumps aboard, I must maintain a life-support system—I am in error. It is possible to shield the ship, but it will take most of the available power."

"Then you'll do it?"

"This is what CaptainHayden wishes me to do?"

"He wants information on Gella Icor and my slither," Sis-Silsis answered.

"I will follow you to Halmarin-IV," Deso answered.

"Will Drumps object?" Sis-Silsis wanted to be sure he could count on Deso's monitoring before he left the big ship there.

"He has two new atmospheric mixtures to study and does not wish to be disturbed," Deso replied. "I will not intrude on his work."

Sis-Silsis decided Deso had a devious mind for a robot, but he kept his thoughts to himself. If he let the droid know what he thought, Deso might decide to ask Drumps if he approved, and the scientist was a strange creature to the cynbeth. Better the human continued his work in peace.

Sis-Silsis caught up on his sleep while the ship was in time-comp. He checked his brood, ordered Hercules to charge his empty storage registers, and was pacing the lounge, scattering his slithers right and left, when the klaxon sounded to bring them back into normal space.

He hurried to the cockpit, shutting his progeny in the lounge, and was ready when they came out of time-comp. He expected to cross the Halmarin system as he came out of comp, and come back to normal space with the two ships between the settled planets.

He did not expect to be blind in all sensors, or to have his copilot go berserk and start grabbing at air.

"Hercules-s, s-stop that and raise—"

Sis-Silsis was interrupted by the droid, who started to whistle an off-tone, earsplitting sequence of five notes repeated over and over. He kept grabbing, his huge metal fist clasping air just above the cynbeth's shoulder.

"What in seven stars is going on?" Sis-Silsis demanded, raising the screen himself and staring out. He wasn't where he was supposed to be. Judging by the brown swirls below him, he was just above Halmarin-IV's atmosphere. Just off to the side, *Windsong* became visible. The Deso had been honed in on him, so the glitch that brought him out in the wrong place had also brought the Skooler ship.

But something was wrong aboard *Windsong*. The ship was jinking, or as close to it as something that large could come. It was rolling from side to side, and moving down toward the atmosphere.

"Deso!" he shouted into the comm-link and grabbed the emergency set of earphones from the recess next to his seat. He would never be able to hear over the noise Hercules was making. "Deso! Answer me!" he ordered, knowing there was no need for stealth and radio silence. The Halmarins had to know they were there.

"Deso!" he called again, but the receiver was giving off so much static that if the droid answered, he couldn't hear anything else. Finally he caught the whistle through the static, the same five notes Hercules was making.

When Sis-Silsis realized what was wrong, his skin shivered, causing a clatter of the hard scales on his back. He had come into the magnetic storm region. He had heard about it, but had never paid much attention, since reptiles habitually stayed away from the sectors of space frequented by the Halmarins.

The storms had glitched the ship's computer, and Hercules and . . .

"Deso! Call Drumps to fly you out!" he shouted. His only answer was that frantic string of notes.

"Deso! Call Drumps!" he shouted again. He kept calling as he watched the ship sink lower into the atmosphere. Even knowing his danger on the planet, he could not stop himself from following the huge black vessel down. He had to stay close, to get through to the droid.

Conek had told him the larger Skooler units had small self-correcting systems for minor malfunctions. Sis-Silsis had to be near enough to be heard if Deso was able to correct the reaction of the magnetic disturbance long enough to get the human pilot to the controls.

"Deso, can you hear me?" he shouted again. "Damn you, answer me!" Cynbeth did not swear in the human style, but Conek Hayden did. He was hoping the familiarity would reach the droid's computer.

"Eat him up!"

"How did you get in here? Get off that control panel." He reached for Gisar, grabbed him just before he settled on the firing controls, and tossed him back toward the rear of the cockpit.

The little slither spread his wings, soared up, around Hercules's reaching arms, and landed on the droid's knees. Sis-Silsis made a grab for the green-gold, ducking under the droid's reaching hands, but while he was trying to reach Gisar, two blue-golds came through the door and decided it would be fun to land on the swinging black metal arms and get a free ride.

In the meantime *Destria* was moving down at too fast a rate, and if he didn't control the ship, the dangerous angle of entry into the atmosphere could do serious damage and possibly burn it up. He threw up the force wall just as the outside hull started sending off heat vapors.

"Deso, get your shields up!"

He couldn't tell if the droid had heard him. Without sensors he couldn't tell if the shields were up on *Windsong* or how far they were from the surface.

As the two ships descended, he discovered the brown atmosphere continued and became a heavy dust storm. It reached up to the stratosphere, but was it close to the ground? He slowed his speed, staying a hundred meters above the Skooler ship. If he caused the crash of Conek Hayden's largest vessel, at least he would try not to crash *Destria*.

But he wouldn't let *Windsong* crash if he could help it. He kept shouting to Deso, giving him orders to put the ship on automatics, and call Drumps.

"Eat him up!"

The slithers were interpreting his shouting to be anger. Anger meant an enemy.

"Eat him up!"
"Eat him up!"
"Eat him up!"

They chanted in unison while Hercules continued to put out his earsplitting whistle, the brown dust cloud thickened as they neared the surface, and all the monitors showed heavy static.

Then a strong gust of wind parted the dust for a moment and Sis-Silsis saw the squat city buildings, less than a hundred meters below *Windsong*.

The huge ship was still slowly descending.

CHAPTER 15

Lesson swore and drew back his arm to throw the hand communicator across the cockpit. Then he thought better of it. No use in ruining what was probably a working piece of equipment. He stored it in his pocket. It was that damn Griffin and its *fits*.

None of his instruments were working properly, and he had had to order Sleepy, his emergency droid pilot, to shut down.

Lesson glared in the direction of the big Skooler robot, dividing his anger between the droid for not working, Conek for insisting that he take the unit aboard his ship to act as an emergency pilot, and at himself for getting used to having someone to talk to. Some*thing*, he amended. Funny how a body got to thinking of them as alive. He wondered if there was something in their programming that caused it, and if it was a deliberate Skooler plot, something to do with a future invasion.

"I'm letting my mind run away with me," he told the droid, conveniently ignoring the fact that Sleepy couldn't hear him.

It was his own fault that he forgot to warn Ister to be on the lookout for Halmarin patrol ships when they searched

Laver. But the Orelian had never been stupid. He'd keep a close watch.

Lesson prepared to comp.

He wanted to be well out of the Franig system when he came out of time. He might have the reputation of a hot pilot, but he wasn't a fool and knew he couldn't trust his computers in a solar magnetic storm.

Going in at all was foolhardy, but after he'd heard what could happen to little Gella, he knew they had to try. He would have been several times dead if old Icor hadn't helped him out. Lesson paid his debts.

Conek had sent them out to ask questions about CDs, but it didn't take Lesson long to decide the ship they were looking for was going to be unknown in most spaceports. Whoever serviced and repaired it kept his mouth shut out of fear or for good pay.

There was only one way to find it and that was to search for its hiding place, a place where sensors couldn't probe. That meant sight searching, the one thing they *could* do during the magnetic storm, since sensors were no good at this time. The mystery ship might even be flying.

Neither Lesson nor Ister had admitted to the other that the task they were taking on was impossible. They couldn't search whole planet surfaces. They hadn't a chance and they knew it, but they were in the area, and had exhausted every other idea. They'd give it a try.

The ship that had been mistaken for Icor's had been on Halmarin, but hell, no one in that stiff-necked bunch of religious nuts would be smuggling. If the vessel had been there, then it had been because of trouble.

If it had been on Halmarin-IV, then it came from someplace close by. The Franig Solar System was the closest, and Laver was the only habitable planet.

They decided to check Laver, concentrating on the mountains, hoping to find a series of caves, similar to Jon Sluggarth's old hideout on Wios.

Laver had recently received a recommendation for colonization, but as yet no one had settled on it. It was a perfect place for a smuggler's base.

When he came out of time, Lesson started to swear again.

"*Anubis*, you jackass, I wanted to be safe, not in the next galaxy!"

He wasn't exactly in Beta Galaxy, but he was too far away from Laver to please him. The magnetic storm was kicking up strong interference on his sensors. It would be suicide to comp too close to the surface. He had to go in the long way.

"And to think I used to hate comping," he told the inactive droid as he threw full power to the thrusters. Even at hyperspeed he would be hours reaching the planet. Hours were precious for Gella. He thought seriously about going back to Agnar-Alpha to report to Conek, but if he did, Ister would be left on his own. No, he had to keep his appointment with the Orelian.

He had covered half the distance when he felt a desperate need to relieve himself. He reached for the automatic switch, knew he couldn't trust it, and settled for the more primitive method of using his belt to tie down the acceleration rods.

"Just stay out of my way," he shouted out to the general area of space in front of the ship and raced back to the needs in his stateroom.

In a series of dashes from the cockpit to the food dispensers he managed to get some food and some feine. He wished he had a good drink and was glad he didn't. He would need all his control to fly a ground search in the mountains without instruments.

When he was finally down through the atmosphere of Laver, he allowed himself a sigh of relief and then his frustration built again. He and Ister had known just enough about the planet to know there were four continents, one at each pole, and one in each hemisphere. He had told Ister he would take the larger continent in the temperate zone, but when he made an equatorial circle, he discovered they were both of nearly equal size.

So which one should he take, and which was Ister searching?

"*Anubis*, baby, I hope Icor's girl doesn't have to depend on us."

Not knowing where to start, or where Ister was, he took

the closest body of land, found a mountain range, and flew as low as he dared, looking for rock formations. The mountains below him seemed to be composed entirely of earth.

He decided they couldn't be, then changed his mind. They were round as if they had been molded by hand. By the weather, he corrected himself. But somewhere on the range there might be rock and caves. He kept going.

Yep, up ahead he saw peaks that were peaks, higher and sharper than the mounds below him.

"Something coming up, Sleepy," he said as they approached the western side of the higher range.

Then something did come up.

The Orelian Lapper.

Ister came racing through a low saddle between two peaks at fighting speed, passing so close to *Anubis* that the Osalt freighter rocked in the turbulence.

Lesson had just reached for the controls to stabilize the ship when Ister was followed by a CD-63 and a Cenovian Firefly, both with oversize engine pods.

The sixty-three went under *Anubis*. The Firefly skittered off to its right and just missed a visit through Lesson's view ports. Both ships were showing weapons. As they cleared the saddle and lined up on the Lapper, the Firefly let go with all its forward weapons.

"Looks like we picked the right range, Sleepy."

The ship was still canting to the right when Lesson yanked the right thruster acceleration rod back and threw the port breaking thruster into full blast.

"No way to treat you, baby, but we just missed formation," Lesson grunted. The freighter shuddered and narrowly missed plowing into the mountainside before slewing to follow the running fight.

Ister had disappeared over the next ridge followed by the others. Lesson caught sight of the Firefly as it streaked across the ridge and dropped into the valley beyond.

Lesson had turned off the artificial gravity of the ship, and he felt his stomach lurch as he swooped up and then down. He made a desperate grab for the controls and slewed again as he discovered he was down in a gorge and heading straight for a cliff of earth and stone.

The far side of the gorge was racing at him when his hands, moving too fast for conscious thought, slewed the ship again, turning it on its side and missed a collision by inches.

"This valley is too narrow for safe flight," Sleepy suddenly spoke with a logic and clarity that startled Lesson after the wild contortions and crazy sounds the droid had been making.

"So tell me something I don't know," Lesson groused as he raised the ship, but not before Sleepy had taken a look at the monitors.

"The others are going south. We are headed north. We are not assisting IstertheOrelian?"

Lesson glanced down at the sensor monitors and saw what the droid had seen. They were in working order and on the rearview monitors he could see the blips of three ships behind him.

"Of all the stupid—Sleepy, shut *down*!"

Lesson threw the ship into a sharp ascent, which would bring them out of their temporary shielding from the magnetic storm. The droid would go crazy along with all the instruments, but at least Lesson knew where the war had gone.

He soared up and rolled, roaring down a good distance behind the two ships that were still racing down the long gorge. Two ships. What had happened to the third one?

Before his identification sensors glitched he called for an identity readout. The two ahead were the locals.

What had happened to Ister?

He slowed and dropped down closer to the surface, searching the narrow valley. They couldn't have made a direct hit on the Lapper, or he would have seen the explosion. Maybe they crippled it.

Had Ister comped out? He wasn't the kind to leave a fight. Lesson wished he could risk reactivating Sleepy so he would have someone—some*thing* to grouse at.

Then he saw the Lapper ahead, coming out of a tributary valley.

"What happened to you?" Lesson demanded, blaming the

Orelian, angry with him now that he didn't have to be concerned.

"I dodged and they didn't follow," the cat-man said, sounding surprised.

Then before Lesson could ask more, they were interrupted by five ships coming up over the ridge just ahead.

"Black hats behind you," Lesson warned, clearing his blasters and making ready to fight.

Lesson cleared his guns, but he wished he was a little higher off the surface. He hadn't been hired by the local law enforcers to take on all the smugglers in the FarArm of Alpha Galaxy, and if these were the ones he was looking for, he wanted to bring in reinforcements.

The object wasn't to kill them, it was to free Gella, he reminded himself.

Shame.

After his frustration he'd enjoy getting down to it with some Balazaro-bound no-good. He said as much to Ister over the short comm.

"Watch it," Ister's voice crackled back. "I'm still doing a little VladPat dodging now and then." That reminded Lesson he wasn't too far away from the contrabanding business himself.

"Just want to stretch my muscles," Lesson grunted and turned his attention to the ships coming in. While he watched two more vessels came in sight over the low ridge.

That was just a couple too many, Lesson decided. Two wasn't even sporting, since Ister's Lapper was as well armed as the big Osalt freighter. Four would be pretty good fun, but seven—no, it was time to leave.

"Let's make for the alternate," he shouted over the commlink, hoping Ister had kept the origin coordinates from their last jump. There was no time to come up with any others.

They could rendezvous in space and work out a new strategy. The trouble would be comping. Because of the magnetic interference and the glitching computers, who knew where they would be when they came out of time, but getting separated was better than getting shot.

Lesson had his hand on the switch that would activate the

time-comp when he thought better of it. His last coordinates had been close in on a planet. He was too close to the surface of Laver for safety, and with the problems they were facing, he could end up seeing his destination from the inside instead of from space.

He needed to scuttle a good way outside the atmosphere, and around to the dark side of the planet to reset his instruments before jumping.

Only the local boys were moving in too fast. He wouldn't have time. Both the CD and the Firefly were faster than his lumbering giant, and the three ships following the first two were gaining rapidly.

He squinted, trying to decide what they were. Without instruments he had to rely on what he could see through the view ports. By the color, another Firefly led the second group. One was an EF-class, Entra-system freighter, and they were fast little ships. He couldn't tell the model, but he recognized it by the light glinting off the exposed angled view port transparencies.

He couldn't tell what the third one was, but the pilot was an idiot if he thought he could hit either the Lapper or the Osalt freighter at that distance.

Lesson was always surprised at the number of pilots who seemed to think a shot would travel as far in an atmosphere as it would in the near vacuum of space.

The fool was not only out of range, he nearly hit the leading Firefly and the CD.

When he shot again, Lesson thought he hadn't learned a lot from his first experience. The first pair peeled off, the Firefly slewed and shot off to the right and the CD to the left.

Behind them the second Firefly followed the first. The other two ships took off after the CD.

While Lesson was wondering what happened the handheld communicator crackled.

"Did I miss something?" Ister asked.

"Think we should catch up and ask them?" Lesson said, glad he wasn't the focus of the attack, but half hoping Ister would say yes. He was primed for a fight and he felt let down.

They had forgotten about the last two ships until Ister hissed over the short distance system, warning Lesson. By the time he looked around, he had no trouble recognizing them.

They were familiar shapes, old Astro-Cruisers, obsolete and no longer used by the Vladmn Patrol. He couldn't see their markings, but he was sure they were registered to one of the local inner-system patrols. They might be old ships but they carried some long-range armament and weren't any slouches on speed. They were too close for him to get away.

"Local legals," he warned Ister. The Lapper could probably make it out, but *Anubis* was too slow.

The ship's comm-link rattled with static.

". . . and disengage thrusters . . ." was all he heard before the crackle blurred the rest. ". . . unarmed . . . hands raised . . ."

"Hell, call me a jackass and fit me for a saddle," he muttered. In more than thirty years of smuggling, he had never been caught in a position where he could neither fight nor run.

"That's what comes of turning honest," he griped and flipped the sending switch on the comm-link.

"Communication garbled, repeat, communication garbled," he shouted. "I am landing now. Repeat, I am landing now."

He slowed his speed and started down in a slow, non-menacing spiral. If he could keep their attention, perhaps Ister could escape and warn Conek. He might need the boss to buy him out of trouble.

No hope for that, he thought as he looked up. Ister had joined his spiral and was following the Osalt freighter down.

CHAPTER 16

Andro accelerated the small ground speeder and zipped into the nearest alley, but he was not quick enough to keep from being seen by the first of the bright green and yellow vehicles racing down the street.

"Blasters ready, my dears," he called over the roar of their own machine and the wailing sirens on the approaching zippers.

"It's my fault," Wiers cried out. "Never should have talked to that lying Doochin . . ."

"Shut him up!" Andro snarled at Nelsf. The alley was littered with cartons and bales of something Andro could not identify. To him they seemed to be random and without order, but they might be used for cover in a firefight. If a person could keep his mind on the battle and wasn't distracted by the glaring pinks and livid greens and purples of the packing cases.

He could understand their need for color on their dull, brown world, but pink and yellow striped shipping cartons?

That's right, dear, you keep on thinking of the trivial, and maybe you'll get the speeder to shelter before you panic completely.

"They didn't stop," Fsith said as he watched their back trail. "So maybe they didn't see us turn. . . ."

"Or maybe Doochin told us the truth and this alarm has nothing to do with us," Nelsf said to Wiers. "They can have any number of troubles in these magnetic storms."

"They're not coming after us," Fsith said as Wiers stretched his segmented body to look over Fsith's carapace. He didn't get a long look. Andro had guided the speeder through the maze of cartons and turned off the first alley into a second. Thirty meters ahead most of its width dead-ended at a large set of orange doors. The narrow section that continued on was less than a meter wide.

At least they had not been followed. He brought the speeder to a halt and sat trying to figure out what to do next. Most important was trying to calm Wiers so they could all think. The doubtful mentot was muttering to himself, sounding as if he'd lose control and start screaming at any minute.

"Sweetie, they could have half the city in trouble," Andro said. "Malfunctioning electronics can cause shorts and start fires—who knows what could be happening. Let them have their panic. If they're too busy to notice us, it's to our advantage."

"We were supposed to hide the speeder anyway," Nelsf suggested, looking around. Ahead they had little choice in hiding places, since the orange doors were their only alternative to leaving the speeder in the alley, but behind them were other entrances to other buildings. None of the doors were open but two on the other side of the intersection were standing ajar.

If there were any workers about, they were staying inside the buildings. According to Doochin, all work but that involving life support shut down during the worst part of the storm period.

"And this may be as good a place as any," Andro agreed. Before he could untangle himself from the controls, Nelsf and Wiers were out of their seats and pattering along the alley. Wiers took the obvious course, going to the doors at the end of the alley. Nelsf went back three meters behind the speeder and checked the partially open entrance.

Andro could see into the warehouse ahead as Wiers pushed one large door to the side. The building was empty. Gelcrin Fruit Shippers, as the sign above the door identified the business, didn't seem to have much trade. They could hide the speeder there, but if anyone opened those doors . . .

"Fluffy bales of fiber, marked for Orser," Nelsf said, pattering back to the side of the speeder. "They won't be shipping until after the storms. We can put the vehicle in there and stack the bales around it."

"And if we have to get out in a hurry . . . ?" Fsith asked. Being strapped onto the back of the machine was beginning to wear on his courage.

"Then we can drive right through them. They're big but they're light."

Ten minutes later they had hidden the speeder in the warehouse and consulted their instructions. While they were still on the ship, Andro had tried to draw a map. He'd done well at cartography in the academy, but without any references other than those Doochin had given him, he didn't have much faith in it.

"We were to go up that street and turn right after three hundred meters," he said, jerking his head to indicate the thoroughfare they had left.

"If this little alleyway will take us that far . . ."

Andro really wished Fsith would finish his sentences. He consulted his map again. They were two kilometers into the city already. They were in the area where Doochin had told them to hide the speeder. The warehouse he had chosen for them was on a side street about three hundred meters up the secondary street they had been traveling when the Halmarins panicked.

The small alleyway was deserted, and the howling wind was not loud enough to cover the blaring sirens on the street.

"On, dear hearts," Andro urged as he gave his blaster one last check and felt his pockets to be sure he had not lost the extra power packs.

Nelsf took the lead, moving ahead of the others. He paused at every door and side passage. Every time he stopped the others pressed themselves to the wall.

When Nelsf reached the next street he paused longer, seemed to be considering, and then crept slowly out, angling off to the right. Andro could understand his direction. Doochin had told them of the narrow foot passages through the city and after they had left the speeder on an adjoining street, they were planning to make use of them. It was the mentots' stealth that surprised Andro.

Fsith was following behind Nelsf and he followed Nelsf's example. Wiers was third in line and he had pulled himself together now that he had some activity to keep his mind occupied.

Andro brought up the rear. He paused at the entrance to the alley and looked out. He could hear voices, apparently they had been the cause of Nelsf's caution, but the heavy dust swirls blowing along the street was like a dense fog. He was halfway across when a sharp gust of wind thinned the dust and he saw the dim shapes of more than twenty Halmarins just off to his left. He froze for a moment, but they were busy looking up and behind him.

Andro wasn't curious about what was holding their attention as long as they didn't notice him. He moved slowly, angling for the alley where he could see Nelsf, Fsith, and Wiers standing in full view, staring like the Halmarins.

He quickened his steps as he came within three meters of the alley entrance and had to step over Wiers who was so caught up in what he was seeing that he didn't notice the major.

With a tall building close on either side, Andro turned to see what fascinated everyone.

At first he could see nothing but dust. Then the strong winds thinned it and he could make out the enormous black, elongated shape. He was seeing a ship, one he recognized, and it was so close to the top of the highest buildings he had trouble believing his eyes.

Windsong was hanging over the city. The ship was rocking from side to side, shifting and yawing as if it were barely in control and ready to crash any minute.

After seeing what had happened to Lovey-I, Andro could believe Deso had also been affected by the magnetic storms.

Madder Drumps was supposed to be aboard, so why hadn't he taken over the controls? Andro didn't think much of Drumps as a pilot, but he wouldn't let the ship hang there, in danger of crashing, if he could help it. Drumps had to be incapacitated in some way.

Andro had to do something about that ship. If it crashed it would be the end of *Windsong*, the pride of Conek's cargo fleet, and after they had gotten over their worries about its size, it was the pride of the Agnar-Alphan spaceport controllers too. To Andro, Deso was nearly human, and there was a human on board. Andro might burn down a Halmarin or two to free Gella, but Major Avvin was Vladmn Patrol. He could not stand by and watch most of a city destroyed.

He felt a need to do something. He didn't have a single idea. Even if he could get aboard *Windsong*, he couldn't fly the Skooler ship. He didn't care about the old CC-12, but he couldn't leave Lovey-I aboard it.

He didn't even wonder why the ship was over Halmarin-IV. Like him, it was there because of Gella.

Gella!

If he could get to her and get her back to the CC-12, there might be some way to get her aboard the Skooler ship. If anyone could figure out the controls and get that ship out, she could.

"Let's go, sweeties." Andro strode off down the narrow alley, leaving the rest to follow. They were protected from the wind by the high, blank electric blue walls, but the dust clouds were as thick as they had been on the open plain. Their eyes were protected by their masks, and they wore breathing filters. The mentots breathed through their sides, and looked as though they were wearing life preservers, and since the rrotta's nostrils were on top of his carapace, he wore his cap style.

Doochin's estimate of the distance between the street where they left the speeder and the building that housed the Ministry of Justice was a little over three kilometers. Andro, after a long series of stops to wait and listen, crossing streets, hurrying down narrow alleys, and repeating the sequence again, thought they had gone a lot farther. He found it hard to judge distance when it seemed that every step he took carried him straight into a brown wall.

Not all the route was through the small, narrow footways. Three times they found themselves in wider alleys and once they had to travel along a street that would ordinarily be crowded with traffic. Apparently Doochin had been right about the Halmarins' habit of staying inside during the windstorms. Though they were out in force, to watch the huge ship and complain about it, they were staying close to the doorways on the north and west sides of the streets. There was no traffic except for the siren-screaming official cars.

Andro led the way down a wide alley that could have been a boulevard on some worlds. Then he realized his were the only footsteps he could hear. He paused. Nothing. Cold prickles danced up his spine.

What had happened to the others?

Then he heard a soft pitter-patter and Wiers appeared out of the dusty fog.

"Major Avvin, sir. We've found some food for Fsith."

"Food for—" Andro stared at the mentot, wondering if he was in some nightmare. This couldn't be for real. They were on a hostile world, creeping about in a cloud of brown dust, Gella had to be rescued, that ship was about to fall on the city, and the rrotta was stopping for lunch?

"Sweetie, that ship up there may fall any minute . . ." And then it might not, and the rrotta had been having a hard time of it, since there had been almost nothing aboard the CC-12 for him to eat.

The mentots shied away from high-protein foods but could eat most human foods. The rrotta were less adaptable. Off their own world, they subsisted mostly on an odorous hash.

Andro had heard it was made of some sort of sea creature, ground up and mixed with a tree-type fibrous plant. As long as it was known that one sentient was not eating another it was considered discourteous to ask. The answer invariably caused the questioner to gag.

He had been thoughtless in not making sure there was something edible aboard the ship for the rrotta, and had been trying to ignore the paling color of the crustacean's carapace, a sign of malnutrition and outright hunger.

"Oh, for—what is it?" He might be sorry he asked that question. "Where is he?"

"Back—" Wiers tried to point and decided it was futile in the dust. "I'll show you."

Andro followed the mentot to a doorway and inside. In the dim light he could tell they were in some sort of live fish shop.

"These are green legords," Nelsf said as he scooped a small net into the water and brought it up, filled with what Andro would have called skinny green fish. He dumped them into a fabric bag. "Fsith says only the poorest people on his planet eat them, but they're better than nothing."

Fsith wasn't saying anything. He was at the second tank. He also had a bag. He alternated by eating one scoop and putting one in the bag he was holding. When Wiers started bagging fish too, Andro objected.

"How far do you think we'll get, leaving a trail of dripping seawater?"

"They won't drip long, and the wind will dry the ground almost immediately," Nelsf answered without breaking his rhythm of scoop and dump.

Andro sighed, picked up a net, and make one pass into the tank. He brought up his catch and with a shudder dropped it, net and all. The larger ones looked more like water snakes. No wonder the rrotta didn't consider them choice items. Then he saw the price list by the crana-coffer. The Halmarins certainly must think they were a delicacy.

"I'll keep watch," he said, going back to the door. He shuddered again, hoping Fsith would eat up his catch in a hurry. Just the idea of those wigglers gave him the shivers.

He looked out in time to get a view of the Skooler ship through a break in the dust clouds. The huge black vessel had moved a little to the north, and was higher, but still yawing as if not under anyone's control. He could just make out the shapes of two Halmarin ships hanging off the port side of the big vessel. They weren't firing, but they wouldn't, not right over the city. They were probably trying to contact the pilot.

What a mess!

Gella was in prison, *Windsong* hung overhead like an evil presence, he was sneaking around a hostile planet where he had no authority—no he wasn't even doing that. He was aiding and abetting a robbery of some expensive little green snakes.

Why didn't he stay on Agnar-Alpha where he belonged? he asked himself.

"We're ready," Nelsf said, pattering up to the door. He was carrying a dripping sack that undulated; just the sight of it made Andro queasy. The bag wasn't very large, but the mentot was using both hands to hold it. Wiers also had one, and while Fsith could manage his with only one hand, he was using the other to pull the wriggling legords out of the bag and stuff them in his mouth. If they needed to fight, Fsith might lose his future meals.

Andro looked away hurriedly before he lost his last one. He could still hear the rrotta crunching.

"Eat a little quieter, dearie," he said, leading the way out of the building.

"It's only the heads that crunch," Fsith answered.

Andro's stomach gave a lurch. "Shut up, will you, love?" He was definitely not meant for this sort of life.

Half an hour later they had reached the next and final stage of their trip across the Halmarin capital city. Andro had hated even hearing about this part of the route. When they crowded together to raise the cap on the sewer maintenance vent he hated it even more.

In comparison he thought he could even stand Fsith's snakefish. The breather masks that kept out the dust weren't adequate for the smell. It didn't help to know that the sewers were relatively free of human excrement and other nonrelated organic waste. Andro suspected the odor came from the densoks, specially bred reptiles that consumed anything organic. Just having to go down there was enough to make him taste bile.

But it was the only way to reach Gella.

He led the way again, following the map. As the advertisements had read, the sewer was relatively clean. A deep channel ran down the middle with half-meter-wide walks on each side.

The walks and the arched tunnel were fused earth, and the lining of the channel had once been white plasteel, but it was green with slime that glittered in the light of his illuminator.

Behind him he heard a splash. The beam from Fsith's light showed the biggest pair of jaws he had ever seen.

Four blasters went off at one time, and the creature sank beneath the surface of the water.

"Made me drop the bag," Nelsf said and Andro turned the light on him in time to see him picking up the spilled legords and stuffing them back into the bag. At least the creatures were dead and no longer wiggling.

"Come on," Andro urged. He made himself a promise. He was never again going on a dangerous mission with mentots and rrotta. He had just turned when another densok reared up out of the channel, the several sets of its eyelids folding back for better vision, and a green slimy growth hanging down from its wide jaws. He blasted it three times before it turned and splashed away down another tunnel.

"Another three minutes and we'll be out of here," Andro said when he heard snufflings and roars from the intersecting channels. He wondered if they would have enough power in their blasters. Just ahead should be the vent that would take them up into the sub-basement of the building that housed the Ministry of Justice and the detention chambers. He shot two more densoks, and walked sideways. More of them were coming up the tunnel behind them. Ahead he saw the ladder that should take them up into the sub-basement. It had to be the one. Doochin had said there would be a sign on it, forbidding entry. To the Halmarins that would be gospel. To the breakers of Halmarin law, it was an arrow pointing the direction.

Andro was the only one with both hands free, so he stayed at the bottom of the tunnel and let Fsith take the lead. As the rrotta passed him, Andro hoped the others would hurry up the ladder. The smell was overpowering. Densoks were supposed to react to odors, but how they could tell there were intruders in the tunnel was more than he could understand.

But they knew. Three were coming up the tunnel at once. He fired four times, and when they fell back beneath the surface he gave Wiers a shove to send him up the ladder.

The blaster was losing power. It stung and momentarily stunned the densoks but they were coming in again. He jumped for the ladder, laying down a spray of fire that was now only momentarily diverting the lizards.

The largest one lunged and nearly had his boot before Andro scrambled up the vent far enough to be out of reach. Fear had drained his strength and he wondered if he could finish the climb. He was surprised when he reached the top of the ladder and pulled himself up onto the stone floor of the sub-basement.

"We'd better close that vent," Nelsf said, suiting actions to words. "The smell will alert the guards."

"You do that," Andro said, though by the time he spoke it was past tense, but it was already too late. The odor was as strong in the dry underground chamber as it had been below.

"Let's get started, but stay together and stay quiet—and, Fsith, I told you, stop that crunching!" He shuddered and led the way out of the small utility room.

Andro led the way down the passages, and had reached the third one before he decided he'd missed a turning somewhere. He needed to reread his directions, and in an open passage was no place to display a map reading light.

He was angry with himself for losing his way, but he remembered the turns he had made, so he led his unlikely team back to the utility room again. He opened the door, held it for the others. When they were inside he pulled out his illuminator, but he didn't get to use it.

He was struck in the face by a sudden blinding light.

"Raise your hands. Don't think of moving."

CHAPTER 17

"You've been using the company Andro and I *vouched* for to smuggle addictives, Captain Hayden?"

For nearly a full minute after Quinta Norden asked her question, the four people in the lounge aboard *Bucephalus* were as still as if they had been frozen.

Conek felt as if he had been. He thought he could not have been colder in muscle and emotion if he'd been in the blackness of space. Strange, his mind seemed crystal clear, surrealistically clear.

The spell was broken by the ragged man Skielth had brought aboard. He started to shake and his knees gave way. He was saved from a hard fall by the Shashar's grip on his arm.

Conek gazed at him as if he were something in a bad dream, unwanted but unreal, and nothing to be concerned about. His mind was on answering the quinta. He turned to face her.

"I suppose you were searching for addictives the first time you came aboard this ship? If I remember correctly, you weren't adverse to my doing a little extra-legal work then, and you didn't ask what else I was shipping."

The first time he had met Quinta Norden she and Quinta

121

Bentian had boarded his ship with the intention of hiring him. Working for them had nearly cost him his life.

Norden had the grace to blush, but she wasn't cowed. "If you remember I was not in favor of the idea, even though I knew what you were carrying—then."

"And you can know now." He tossed her his pocket computer that held his company files. "Look at them and think what you want, but ask yourself if I'd risk Icor's daughter. No, *look*," he demanded when she started to lay the little computer aside. "You might see something I haven't, and if you can find anything that gives us a lead on this mess, I don't care if you accuse me of infanticide."

It was a good boast, anyway—unless he had stepped on one of Sis-Silsis's slithers.

"And fighting with each other, we're missing the point. What have you found out?" The question was addressed to Skielth.

The Shashar told them about his search and the ambush.

"This thing out of a Grevotan slime pit has something to say." He leaned over his captive. "You talk or I'll burn a hole through you." He parted his lips slightly and drew in a slow deep breath.

Conek watched. If the situation had not been so serious it would have been funny. Many worlds had legends about large reptiles that could breathe fire. It seemed strange to him that educated people who would have scoffed at the idea in general conversation often showed their primordial fear when faced with a Shashar leaning over them and taking a deep breath. They seemed to be more threatened by that mythical and nonexistent inner fire than they were of a blaster.

"I didn't *do* anything," the man whined. "I didn't try to kill him. He said himself my blaster was wrecked."

"Who are you?" Norden asked.

Conek nodded. Typical government thinking. First get a name to put on the file.

"Rivlean Pikten, from Orser," he muttered after a hesitation and a scared look in Skielth's direction. "I was just supposed to follow any stranger and see what he was up to. Then I was to trail him back to the spaceport and get the number of his ship." He looked up defiantly. "I wasn't to do anything else, but they gave me a blaster for if I got in trouble."

"Some blaster." Skielth pulled an old weapon from his pouch and threw it to Conek who caught it gingerly, desperately trying to keep his hands off the trigger.

Norden had jumped back on the lounger, tucking her feet under her. She lost three shades of color.

"Skielth! Are you crazy?"

Conek immediately noticed the lack of expected weight. He flipped the catch that opened the weapon for repairs and replacement of the power cell. It not only lacked a power supply, half the triggering mechanism was gone.

"Nothing to fear, Quinta." He offered her the open blaster and let her see for herself. It didn't take her three seconds to recognize the weapon's defects and even less time to understand the meaning behind it.

"You know you were sent out on a suicide mission, Rivlean?"

"I don't see how that could be. I wasn't to use the blaster."

"They told you not to, but how many io-heads would have used the gun to take in a few cranas while they were at it?"

"Who said I was on io?" Rivlean asked, looking around the room. "I never said so."

"Iocineil leaves marks on its users." Norden said. "Those purple marks around your mouth and eyes give you away."

Skielth started another of those deep breaths and Conek formulated a homegrown philosophy behind the man's fear. Sane people who wanted to live in society didn't normally go around shooting people with blasters. But if fire had been a part of the Shashar's inner capabilities, would they have considered using it in the same light as a hand-held weapon? Whether he was right or not, the threat loosened Pikten's tongue.

"I didn't have to do no robbing. They promised me if I told them what I learned . . ." He paused, shook his head as if he had suddenly become aware his failing mental capabilities were showing, and tried again. "*If* I told them what I discovered, I'd be set for a year—" He looked up with a defeated look in his eyes. "If I'd tried to rob the Shashar, I'd be dead. Why would they want me dead?"

"Then they could have gotten the information without paying for it," Norden answered crisply. "Center has an efficient law enforcement service. The authorities would have arrested Skielth for killing you and impounded his ship until they finished their investigation. It would be easy to break into the ship and get any information in the computers. Perhaps the ship as well."

"I didn't ask them for a year's supply," Pikten muttered. "I didn't ask to take io at all in the beginning," he moaned.

From what Conek had heard no one did. Iocineil wasn't a fun drug a user took for kicks. The peddlers of the stuff introduced a bacteria into the systems of their victims without their knowledge. It induced a mental and physical rot, slowed by the taking of iocineil. The victims paid all they had, and then resorted to robbing, killing, and even infecting friends to get relief from the pain.

Iocineil was a new scourge. It had only been discovered five years before. The Vladmn labs had produced a serum that would kill the bacteria, but the victims were usually on the FarArm worlds, and they were told by the pushers that the cure didn't work. They were warned that if they defected to the authorities and tried the serum, they would lose their supply of iocineil. By the time they were desperate enough to try the Vladmn cure they were usually criminals.

"I don't know anything about iocineil," Conek complained.

"Rivlean is going to tell us about it," Norden said. "If he tells us the truth, I'll see to it he gets cured. He won't need the drug anymore. The DCF has a perfect record with io-heads."

She was holding out an empty inducement, since the law demanded the user be turned over to a Dependency Cleansing Facility, but Rivlean apparently didn't know that. He expressed his doubts, but without his supplier, he didn't have much choice. Norden repeated her promise, and added the inducement of giving him a new set of identity papers and having him sent to one of the agricultural worlds in Beta Galaxy where his suppliers would never find him.

While Norden had been making her promises, Pikten had apparently been taking in the fact that he had been set up. He jacked up his mental and physical energies and let loose with everything he knew about the suppliers, the trade in general, and how iocineil was made. He spewed it out with the urgency of taking revenge on the people who had addicted him. When he finished, he collapsed on the lounger, so exhausted with his pain he was nearly unconscious.

When he had started his story, Conek had grabbed a small voice recorder and turned it up to maximum volume. When Pikten collapsed, Conek and Skielth took him down to Norden's zipper with orders for Lieutenant Marwit to take him to the nearest DCF facility. Marwit also carried with him a coded message from Norden to the president of the planetary council on Vilarona, warning him of the small base tucked away on one of the uninhabited islands.

When Conek and Skielth returned to the lounge on *Bucephalus*, they found Norden busy at the computers, feeding in the information.

"At least we know why they wanted him dead," Norden said when they returned. "They'd used him too much."

"And he knows more about their business than they do," Skielth rumbled. "From their point of view, they were stupid not to have killed him themselves."

"I guess they thought they could make use of him one more time, only he was more dependable than they thought," Conek said.

"And more honorable," Norden added. "They expected him to use the gun. It was their bad luck that they didn't realize a dependable tool remains steady."

"Anyway, we have names and locations" Skielth said, trying to hide his impatience with the philosophy. "We've got a starting point."

"Not that it'll do us much good," Conek replied, "They know we have Pikten. They know we got everything from him he could tell us, probably by torture."

"Vladmn does not torture people," Norden snapped.

"No, but *they* would, so that's how they think. They'll already be moving their base of operations. That's not what's bothering me at the moment. There's something I should remember and I can't."

Skielth gave a snort of impatience. "I can't understand what would bother you. Icor is accused of being a murderer, Gella and that cynbeth slither are supposed to be executed, you've been accused of smuggling addictives, but everything else is fine."

"It's not *fine*!" Conek snarled. "Something is definitely wrong! Quinta, punch up the list of chemicals Pikten said they used in making iocineil. Find out exactly what they are."

Three minutes later Norden gave him his answer.

Berecine.

Berecine was a polyglot of chemicals in itself. When they were first mixed they were stable, but aged quickly into a liquid explosive; one of the most powerful explosives known to date. It was legally limited to use only in certain atmospheres. In others it became so volatile it would explode by the building pressure in its container or by contact with chemicals that made up certain breathable atmospheres.

Berecine was made on only one planet; Agnar-Alpha.

All three turned toward the narrow passage that led from the lounge to the cockpit and nearly trampled each other trying to get back to where Norden had left the small computer that held Conek's record of pickups and deliveries.

They had crowded in, but Norden, who had grabbed the file, had not had time to activate it when they saw the official zippers pulling up beside the ship.

Six heavily armed men and an officer piled out and ran to position themselves around the lounge gravator.

The comm-unit crackled with a breathless voice. The officer standing between the guards and holding a hand communicator looked as if he were afraid of his job.

"Captain Conek Hayden. Please come out unarmed."

"Why?" Conek demanded. "With that many guards, you're here to arrest me. For what?"

"There is a question of illegal shipping," the officer replied and then seemed to decide he had volunteered too much. He bit his lip, and apparently thought he should make an effort to ease the situation.

"More than likely it's a mistake, but we have our orders. If you'll accompany us to headquarters and answer some questions."

"Questions, my last shedding," Skielth muttered. "They'll put you in the cell so far back in the jail no one's remembered it in the last century."

"Skielth's right," Norden said slowly. "You can't give yourself up. At least we'll know who we want if we can get a look at that complaint."

"You can do that, but how do I get off Agnar-Alpha?" Conek asked, already searching for an idea. He knew he'd find one. Would it work was the question.

"We'll just burn our way through this bunch and take off," Skielth muttered. He had pulled his blaster and was checking his charge.

"No, you won't," Norden said. She leaned back to stare up at the huge Shashar. "I won't have our men shot up when they're just following orders."

"You know Hayden won't have a chance with his record," Skielth said.

"He will if he can get off Agnar-Alpha and get the proof he needs to clear himself."

"It ought to be one hot ride," Conek muttered, knowing it was his only chance, but every Vladmn Patrol ship in the area would be after him, guns blazing.

"Not if you do what you've done before," Norden said. "You're already known for taking hostages, and no one will shoot at you with me aboard."

"Oh, no." Conek wanted to save his life, not permanently endanger it. "Andro was a major. You're a quinta. It's not quite the same."

"You needn't worry, I'll tell them the truth after we've cleared this up, but we have to get after that berecine. People will die if we don't find it before it goes active."

"Taking you would throw all of Vladmn into a panic," Conek objected, but he'd known the quinta long enough to know once she'd made up her mind he had lost.

"You don't think they would be fool enough to make it public as long as there was a chance I was still alive, do you?"

Conek was right. He had lost.

"Am I a hostage?" Skielth asked. "Don't like leaving my ship."

"No, I'll have to put you off, so you can pass my threat along to those trigger-happy planet pounders," Conek said. "They may not know the quinta is aboard."

It took twenty minutes of conversation over the hand communicators before the guards stationed around the ship moved back and let Skielth off the ship. From the cockpit, Conek and Norden watched as the Shashar hurried over to the captain in charge and started a hurried explanation. Skielth's short arms waved and he shook his head from side to side as he talked.

"He should go in for theatrics," Norden said. "He'd be a holo star in no time."

"From what I can make of his motions, I must have gone over the edge, totally insane," Conek grumbled.

Ten minutes later the comm-unit squawked. Norden answered, sounding breathless, and did a credible job of communicating fear. By the time Conek had warmed the thrusters, they had their clearance to leave the planet.

Norden argued when Conek ordered her back into the lounge, telling her she couldn't very well take the copilot's seat, since she might be seen. When they were in space and into time-comp, Conek made two sudden exits from time. As he expected, they had been followed. He went in and out of time too fast for his pursuers to home in on him. The second time he returned to normal space they had it to themselves as far as the sensors could reach.

Back in the lounge, Norden had been checking Gella's pickup schedule for her last run.

"Gella picked up one shipment on Agnar-Alpha. Precidine

to be shipped to Vilarona. Shipper, one Lagon Fellerd." She looked up, her eyes dark. "Precidine is made on the big island by Alpha-chem. So is berecine."

"Slick setup," Conek said. "If they're caught they can claim it was a mistake in shipping."

"Or you've got someone there in their pay and used the precidine for cover," Norden said.

"Now look, I told you—"

"Conek!" She stared at him wide-eyed. She never allowed herself to get familiar enough to use his first name.

"How—how many containers were aboard *Starfire*?"

"Twenty-six. Damn, that would make some explosion."

"It could destroy the whole solar system," she whispered.

Conek frowned, unable to hide his disbelief. Sure, that much berecine could make quite a hole, and there wouldn't be enough of Gella's ship left to identify, but the quinta was overreacting. She was under too much strain.

Norden saw his reaction.

"I'm *not* losing my mind. During the early space explorations they made every test they could before sending colonists out, but they weren't very thorough by our standards. They could only judge the new worlds by Earth's standards. They didn't realize there were worlds with very thin crusts that did not have volcanic activity."

"Who's skinny in the surface?" Conek asked, but didn't need to be told.

"A lot of worlds in the FarArm of Alpha Galaxy. They were some of the first settled. After the first blasting on Halmarin-IV they banned all explosives from those planets. We have no idea what the berecine could do. If it opened up a large fissure on one of those thinly surfaced planets . . ."

"Another Friday system."

Friday system no longer existed. Seventy years before, one of the planets had exploded. No one knew why. The chain reaction that destroyed the other six planets had taken fifty years, but for twenty years the star, Friday, had been without satellites any larger than small asteroids. Scientists moaned their lack of information. A superstition had evolved and nothing was named after a day of the week, a month, or anything pertaining to a date.

"There are billions of people on some of those old planets," Norden said.

"And very little time to find that berecine," Conek said.

CHAPTER 18

"Move and I'll cut you in half," the voice out of the darkness had said.

"Dear heart, you've said that before," Andro replied. "And moreover, it's not very considerate of you to escape when we were on the way to rescue you."

"Andro!"

"Who else but your knight sans his metal suit, which would have rusted coming through the sewer—I bet they *did* rust too."

Andro recognized his chatter as a nervous reaction and struggled to stop it. He turned his light on wide beam. All four species blinked in the sudden light. The two mentots were momentarily nearly blind, since it took their eyes longer to adjust. The little cynbeth, sitting on Gella's shoulder, tucked his head under her chin.

"I got out by myself, but I still need to get off world," Gella said, wrinkling her nose. "Thanks for coming after me, but why did you bring sacks of dead legords? Were you planning on stifling the Halmarins to death?"

"Is that what I smell?" Andro demanded of Fsith. "I thought it was the sewer!" He thought back and decided Gella

131

had to be wrong. "They didn't have any odor when we got them."

"Then you must have taken them alive, directly from the water," Gella said. "It doesn't take long for them to begin to stink once they're in the air."

Nelsf pulled his bag off his shoulder, loosened his breathing filter, and took a deep breath. He gave a shudder that threatened to separate his segments.

"You didn't tell us about this," he accused Fsith.

The rrotta's clawed feet made small scraping sounds as he moved to look at each face in turn. Not liking what he saw he sank down, his wide carapace just centimeters from the floor, his six long-jointed knees sticking up around him.

"I've never understood this olfactory sense, as you call it," Fsith said. He lowered his sack to the floor, pawing gently at it with one clawed foot.

"Maybe I've eaten enough so I won't starve," he murmured, his translator dripping pathos.

Andro wanted to say the safety of five people demanded leaving the stinking sacks behind, but he was having a little trouble telling the rrotta he could just go hungry again. Fsith's blatant plea for sympathy had worked on his mentot friends.

"He has to have food," Wiers said, his voice rising.

"We'll carry it and stay back where the smell won't bother you," Nelsf said, looking behind him as if he had already been left to his doom.

Andro looked from face to face and shook his head. "When we're back on the ship, you'll keep those—things—in the back hold," he said, pulling out his blaster and checking the charge. "Now, sweetings, I think we had better get out of here before they discover Gella is missing."

He gave the order of march; Fsith with his superior night vision would lead. Nelsf would follow, then Gella, Wiers after her, and Andro would bring up the rear. The mentots had to be protected, since they were nearly blind in the dark.

He opened the hinged lid on the service vent and went down first to stand guard while the others made their descent. Gella remained at the top, shining her stolen light down on the ladder to allow the mentots to see the ladder rungs.

Fsith had reached the tunnel floor and was waiting for the others when a splash up ahead warned them a densok was close. Andro flashed his light and shot at the huge mouthed creature that was lunging for the rrotta. Fsith was hurriedly scrambling back toward the ladder when Andro heard a scrabble of claws on stone behind him and threw himself against the wall. The lunging head missed him by centimeters and he shot straight into the hollow on the side of the lizard's head.

The densok were hard to kill with one shot, but Andro had been lucky. When the big lizard rolled over and splashed in the flooded center channel he became dinner for two others who reared up out of the water and started tearing him to shreds.

"Up the ladder!" Andro ordered Fsith who had scrambled back after the first one attacked. The major cursed his luck at having to wait for the rrotta to climb. Fear and clawed feet didn't make for efficient footing. Another densok climbed over the first two feasting lizards, seeking something better at the foot of the ladder. Andro shot twice, but the bone structure of the lizards made them hard to kill.

He scrambled up behind the rrotta, his feet not a half meter above the snapping jaws. The densok pushed his snout up the ladder shaft, the stench of his breath overwhelming even the stink of the legord sack on Fsith's back.

"Stay close to the ladder," Gella shouted and shot down the shaft, narrowly missing the rrotta and Andro. She shot straight into the lizard's mouth. It drew back just long enough for Fsith and Andro to climb out of reach.

When Andro pulled himself up out of the shaft, he sat on the damp filthy floor, too tired to stand.

"If I ever get back to Agnar-Alpha, I am going into my lovely little office and never set foot out of it again," he announced. "I am definitely not the type for derring-do."

"We're not getting out by the sewer," Gella said, ignoring Andro's complaint. "Those stinking legords have brought every densok within the city."

"We can leave them," Fsith said, this time not making any plea for sympathy. "I'd rather be hungry than dead."

"We still can't use the sewers," Andro pointed out. "The smell has already brought them. They may hang around for several days."

Gella leaned against the wall and gazed down at Andro. "Since that path is blocked, did you have any other plan in mind?"

"We've done the best we could," Andro snapped. "I thought we'd done well just to get here!" Obviously that wasn't enough, but he was smarting at his failure and didn't need her pointing it out.

"I know you have and I thank you." Gella sounded sharp too. "If you don't have an alternate escape route, maybe I do." She paused and when no one else offered a suggestion she started explaining what she knew of the situation.

"There's something going on, I don't know what, but the Halmarins are panicking."

Andro told her about the Skooler ship hanging over the city. She seemed surprised that her friends were putting out so much energy to save her.

"It's given us a chance," Gella said. "The guards in the detention sector have deserted their posts. I don't know what it's like on the upper levels, but I know they keep a squadron of small planet hoppers on the roof of this building. Does that give you any ideas?"

"We should free the other prisoners," Wiers said. The look Gella gave him said that was not what she had in mind.

"There aren't any others. Contrary to what I thought, they don't seem to go in for this sort of thing much."

"If you mean let's get out of here by hopper, I'm all for it," Andro said. "Do you know the way to the roof?"

"I think so. I'm not sure. I know which direction they come from when they bring the food and bedding. There's probably a freight gravator. They won't be using it with everyone in a panic."

"Lead on," he said, changing the order of march again. This time Gella would lead and Fsith would take the center position. He'd still be bringing up the rear, following the stench. He sighed, dimmed his illuminator, and opened the door.

Gella led the way. She led the way for half an hour and they had been down the same passage three times before she found the gravator.

"Delightful tour," Andro said, when they finally found it. "Do you think we missed any memorable sights?"

"Should we go back and check?" Gella snapped at him.

Chirk, chirk! The little cynbeth made his opinion known by looking up.

"Quite right, my dear, we should be on our way," Andro said, stepping into the gravator and starting up. As he rose his foot touched Nelsf's head. Below, the others were crowding in too close. If the Halmarins had guards at the top of the shaft, they would be bunched together and easy targets.

Large battles were far easier to plan than small maneuvers. He was going to remember that in the future. He would remember from the safety of his well-appointed office, where he planned to disappear, never again to be seen by mortal species.

Only one Halmarin guard had stayed at his station on the roof, and he was crouched under a hopper, watching the yawing big black ship.

"It's the end of the world," he said to Andro who surprised him. When the major demanded his weapon, the frightened guard handed it over, though the way he was holding it, he could have shot if he had thought of it.

"It's a judgment on us, we've done something we shouldn't, and it's the end of the world."

"Yes, dear one, but you can make it right. You just go over there and sit down."

In the action holos the hero usually burned the bad guy down or at least knocked him out with a blow to the head, but Andro decided he wasn't that sort of hero. The little character was already too scared to do more than shake his loose folds of excess skin. He gazed up at Andro as if the tall human might be the answer to his prayers. Then he walked away and crouched by the wall of the gravator shaft.

When Gella reached the top of the shaft she looked at the guard and frowned at Andro. Then she turned her attention to the hovering ship.

"It's holding on its automatics," she said after watching it for a minute.

"Then it won't crash?" Andro asked. He understood Vladmn ships but he knew nothing about the alien monster that was rocking just to the right and a hundred meters over their heads.

"I don't know it won't," Gella said. "It's this magnetic mess. It's glitched Deso and the ship's computers, and there's no way to tell if they might go down completely."

"I'd hate to see Conek lose that ship," Andro said. "Is there any way we can get it out?"

"We can try," Gella said. "I'd hate to see it fall on the city."

Chirk! Little Red rustled his wings and hissed.

"I know you don't like them, but they aren't such bad people," Gella said, stroking the little red-gold reptile's neck.

"They were going to kill you," Andro reminded her.

"But they didn't like the idea," Gella said. "It isn't a matter of revenge. They believe it's their duty to cleanse my spirit, or soul, or something. Icor's too."

"Uh, could we go?" Nelsf asked, nervously double-timing in place with six of his eight feet. "My filter is clogging up in this dust."

"I don't know what the hurry is," Andro said, shouldering the long-barreled military weapon he had taken from the Halmarin guard and sauntered toward the parked hoppers. "We're only fleeing for our lives, after all. So far we've acted as if we were on a picnic, and we've gone sightseeing, and now we've lost Wiers and Fsith. And I am getting bitchy, bitchy, bitchy."

"But who's noticing?" Gella asked as she leaned into the open cockpit of the first hopper and checked the gauges. "This one doesn't have enough power charge to lift off the pad."

"These are charged up," Wiers called out. He and Fsith had slipped away and by following their voices, the others found them standing by four hoppers that were angled to take off over the side of the roof. Fsith was already crammed in the rear seat of the nearest.

"Then in you go," Andro said to Wiers as he looked around. "We won't all fit in one. . . ."

"We should take all four," Gella suggested. "We can confuse anyone following us."

"Lovely, but since we only have one set of instructions to follow back to our ship . . ."

Behind them they heard a shout. A spray of blaster fire burned a temporary hole in the flying dust.

"Sightseers on the roof!" Gella yelled as she threw back a shot and jumped into the nearest hopper. When she said they should take all four ships, Nelsf, anxious to be away, had run to the farthest one and was already firing up the engine. A second engine fired, and Wiers squealed as it jumped off the landing pad before he had expected to take off.

Gella threw two more shots behind them at random while she started her hopper. Andro added more firepower to hers, hoping to pin their pursuers down. Not much hope when he couldn't see them, he thought. The Halmarins had the advantage because they knew the general location of the hoppers.

When the engine of Gella's hopper caught, it also leapt off the roof. Apparently the Halmarins had them set for emergencies.

Andro jumped into the fourth one and hit the starter switch. The machine came to life, but no lift-off.

"What the hell?"

He looked down at the controls. The acceleration, breaking, and steering rods were the same as on the ground speeder, but they were inactive until he did something else. He looked at the rows of switches and buttons. All unlabeled. The hoppers were Halmarin manufacture, and he couldn't tell stop from go. Over his head the brown dust disappeared in a blaster shot. He threw another shot back over his shoulder and turned to stare at the controls.

"Dearie, you're a button pusher, so push," he urged himself, not knowing what to touch. One switch might shut down the engine, while one might even be a self-destruct button. The hoppers had gun mounts. Hitting the wrong button might send out a shot and hit one of the other hoppers that were somewhere out in front of him.

Behind him, footsteps were pounding on the roof. Two more flashes of fire came sailing over him. One hit the windscreen, shearing off a small corner.

He took a deep breath and flipped a switch. The hopper rose straight up on its antigravs, but hung stationary. At least the Halmarins were shooting under him now. He flipped another switch at random and nearly snapped his neck as the hopper shot forward. He hastily angled up. He had no idea how tall most of the city buildings were, and he could be on a collision course with the mayor's office, or the central location for the city dump, since nothing the Halmarins did made much sense to him.

At least he was away from that roof. Now if he could only find—

"Yiee!" He gasped as he nearly made a quick visit into the rear of another hopper. As he passed he saw Nelsf's frozen expression of fear. It occurred to him to wonder if the mentot knew anything about flying hoppers. The two mentots and the rrotta had been in the ground patrol on Agnar-Alpha.

Another hopper nearly sideswiped him and he saw Gella whiz by with Wiers so close over the rear of her little ship that the two looked connected. He just had time to notice the thin hair on the mentot's head was streaming back, making him look as if he had ears, and Fsith in the back—*eating* again.

Gella had angled off to the left before she was out of sight in the dust, and as Andro turned his head, wondering if he should follow, he saw Nelsf behind him, his hopper nearly touching Andro's ship. No fast turns, or they would be riding pick-a-back, he decided.

Then Gella came in sight again, pacing her flight just off his right.

Fine, they were all lined up. Now what did they do? Should they try to board the Skooler ship, or get back to their own vessel?

Charging out of that dust into the side of the big black ship wasn't his idea of a fun afternoon of planet hopping. Getting back to the abandoned spaceport in the mountains would be next to impossible when he couldn't get close enough to the ground to follow the landmarks. Doochin hadn't given them any instructions for leaving the city by hopper.

"Idiot, you have a compass," he reminded himself. With one hand still on the controls he pulled it out and studied it, angling to port as he tried to get on an easterly course. The dust was affecting his judgment, he decided. He thought he was turning, but east was still off to the right. Something must be wrong with the steering mechanism, he decided a minute later. East was *still* off to the right! He tried again, with the same result.

Then what he thought was a distant rumble of thunder sounded over the noise of the engine and he looked up. Gella was flying beside him, staring at him as if he had lost his mind. She didn't need to say a word. He stared down at his direction finder. The damn thing was magnetic! He threw it down onto the floorboards and stared out at the dust. He'd been flying in circles, and had managed to lose his direction entirely!

Suddenly in front of him loomed the huge shape of the Skooler ship. He threw the hopper into a steep climb to avoid a collision. The small engine roared and sputtered. The black lusterless skin of the alien ship seemed to be racing to meet him. The hopper stalled and caught just in time to prevent a collision. He just made it over the top and looked back to see if the others had cleared it.

Their engines were sputtering, but they had followed Andro over the top. He was just giving a sigh of relief when he saw Conek Hayden.

The name stood out in huge letters on a white background, and off to his left he was dimly aware of "wner," much dimmer in the dust cloud. As he forced the hopper into a steeper climb, "den Hau" leapt at him in larger, clearer, blacker letters. He just shaved past them when the overstrained engine cut out and he thumped down on the top of an Osalt freighter.

Behind him he heard the scrape of metal against metal and Nelsf's hopper went sliding past him, the landing gear bent, and the bottom of the little ship seemed to be caved in. Andro spared a quick look at the top of the giant spaceship. Conek wasn't going to like that dent, but the hopper hadn't ruptured the hull.

The hoppers Gella and Wiers were flying had stronger engines, but when they saw the other two ships down, they hovered just above. Gella eased her vehicle down beside Andro, keeping the engine going.

"Anyone else here we don't know about?" she shouted.

Andro ignored the flip remark as he restarted his engine.

"Is there any way to get inside from the top?"

"Not that I know of! Look out!" Gella shouted as she shot forward. The freighter was going into a slow roll, and Nelsf's damaged hopper was sliding away. While Andro babied the overheated engine into rising and followed, Gella moved in to hover by the downed hopper. Nelsf didn't forget the bag of legords when he climbed into the seat behind her.

When Nelsf was aboard, she eased over the top of the freighter and dropped down in front of the cockpit view port. Keeping one hand on the controls, she started motioning with the other. The only gesture Andro understood was the one she made to him to follow her. She led the way beneath the ship. Wiers was just behind him when they reached the third and largest hold, and the big lower doors opened.

The hoppers were small enough to pass through. When all three had settled to the deck, Gella climbed out of hers and went to the wall, where a touch of a switch closed the doors again.

Gella led the way forward until they were in the forward hold and ready to enter the lounge.

"This is where the danger comes in," she said with a grin. "You're in more danger here than you were with the Halmarins. Go in quick, but don't make a false step."

Andro would have explained to the mentots and the rrotta but Gella didn't give him time. She opened the hatch, and his part of the operation was to rush the others through and get to the controls on the other side.

Luckily the more than three hundred slithers who occupied

the lounge weren't expecting the door to open and before they could reach it, Andro had hurried across the floor and closed off their escape.

Fsith and the mentots stood in the middle of the lounge, looking around in disbelief. The rrotta had unfolded his long legs and was stetched up to his full height. The mentots were trying to watch both sides of their long segmented bodies at the same time, trying to make sure none of their six mobile feet came down on the slithers.

Andro and Gella worked their way through the mass of little cynbeth that nearly covered the floor of the short passage leading to the cockpit. Sis-Silsis was at the controls. In the copilot's seat, Hercules was still waving his arms, but the glitched command had him grasping air and he had ceased to function.

"I'm not paying for that hull damage," Sis-Silsis announced. Andro noticed he was not looking at the ceiling but at the little slither that was still riding on Gella's shoulder. "And if you want to get out of here, you'd better think of some way to get aboard that ship and take the controls from that glitched droid," he added.

"No hello, I'll break your neck for endangering my slither, or glad to see you're not dead?" Gella asked with a grin.

"Time for that later," Sis-Silsis said, and gave a series of hisses. Little Red lifted off Gella's shoulder and flew over to land on his father's back.

The ship was still rolling, and they heard a screech of metal that came to an abrupt stop. The damaged hopper had slid off the top of the ship.

"I could have been up there," said Nelsf, who had gingerly followed them.

"Didn't know who it was," Sis-Silsis explained. "For the last few minutes the sky's been full of hoppers; at least four have gone down in head-on collisions."

"I thought they'd be chasing us, but we didn't see any," Andro said.

"We wouldn't," Gella retorted. "The last thing they expected was for us to go into a circling pattern."

"And you thought I didn't know what I was doing," Andro said, hoping she had not seen the compass.

"The next question is, how do we get aboard *Windsong*," Gella said.

"No, the next question is, *what is that stench*?" Sis-Silsis demanded.

CHAPTER 19

Lagon Fellerd didn't regret setting a meeting in the public natural growth area of the city, but he could have wished it had not been on the general recreation day. He could have wished the weather was not so bright and sunny. The light bothered his eyes and kept him from concentrating.

It seemed unjust that after spending so much time underground on Agnar-Alpha, he would come out to a surface world and find real sunlight to glare at him.

The natural growth area was a misnomer. The plants and trees that grew there were real enough, but they were not natural to the world of Cornstalk. He wondered morosely if they were natural anywhere, since their origins were from old Earth. The first settlers terraformed planets, but there was always a difference in chemically worked soils. The next generation was always slightly different from the original transplants. These had come from a series of different worlds, and if anyone had kept count of the number of minor mutations they had undergone, Fellerd had never read of it.

He had once viewed a holo information film on Earth flora and fauna. These tall, spindly posts with their long, slanting branches and sparse leaves did not resemble anything he had seen in that holo.

On Earth the trees had stood in solitary splendor. These clustered tightly together in groups of six or seven as if they needed each other to remain upright. Their limbs intertwined, binding them together, and the best thing that could be said for them was their small, spindly leaves provided some relief from the glaring sun.

Fellerd didn't like nature, natural or otherwise. He needed it and the crowds it drew for safety.

The area was crowded with most of the species that lived in Gladtown, the sprawling capital city of Cornstalk. Most had their offspring with them. A dozen little txorch were tussling on the paved walk. Even the newly-hatched liked to fight. Fellerd paused, not quite sure he could step over the minor battle, and decided to take a shortcut, crossing the short blue-green growth that served for grass on the planet.

He was within thirty meters of the walk again when he was surrounded by young mentots who had abandoned their own quieter game to chase a ball thrown by a young human. Mentots did not grow their body hair until they were nearing maturity. The hatchlings were off-white, their bare skin glistened wetly, resembling the larva of the porlynons, the ancestral insectival enemies of his species.

He shuddered as he extended his long legs to step over them and then forgot them for a real menace waiting just ahead.

The human-looking creature in the light blue tunic and pants wore a pair of human-style boots. Fellerd wondered how his feet—if he had feet—fitted in them. The half-breed wore an oversize pair of light-refracting goggles and a sun-shading hat that gave him the appearance of being a Sanulin. The humanoids of that world were reputed to be quiet, meek-natured people who had developed a sensitivity to light after centuries in their subsurface society.

There was nothing meek about this creature, and it was because of his nature that Fellerd had chosen a public meeting place.

At least Onetelles could not kill him there, not if he wanted to remain unknown. Since he was under indictment by every planetary government in the tri-galactic federation, Onetelles had to be careful.

During the rebellion that had erupted when the Amal—the Amalgamation of Mining Industries—had tried to take over the space government of Vladmn, Onetelles had been their hatchet man. When they were overcome and destroyed, the stories of the half-breed's brutalities had come out. Millions had died at his command. Nearly the entire population of Quinta Norden's ancestral planet of Delevort had been destroyed by his order.

Since the rebellion, there had been frightening rumors of an entire planet of creatures like Onetelles; some sort of genetic experiment that had created monsters. Fellerd didn't know whether to believe the story or not. He just wished he had never agreed to the contracts that had brought him in contact with the Amal's ex-hatchet man.

Fellerd approached the two molded seats where Onetelles sat on one, his feet propped up in the other to keep away any idler who might overhear their conversation.

"You're late." The half-breed's words were short and clipped, like the clicks of an insect. He was reputed to be half txorch. Fellerd believed it.

The cleosar waved one exoskeletal front leg in the direction he had come, indicating the crowds. If Onetelles had been sitting on the bench more than a minute before Fellerd had seen him, then he knew Fellerd had crossed the most crowded part of the nature area.

Fear caused Lagon Fellerd to stutter and stammer as he explained the lost shipment.

Onetelles watched the trembling creature as he talked, listing all the unforeseen incidents that had occurred.

"You couldn't have known the Olynthr councilor would want a favor that would put us in such a mess."

Onetelles didn't speak. He stared out at the crowds and tried to keep his mind off the fat little bodies playing on the grass. Safety had made it imperative that he limit his appetite while he was in hiding, and food was always on his mind.

But he could see so much clearer than these limited single-species beings. Of course the Olynthr would want favors, and it had been up to Fellerd to limit the type he gave, always exacting a price.

The cleosar was stupid. He would have to be exterminated, but not quite yet. There was still too much to do.

The small group he had brought off Kayarsit-III was working out well. They were all half-breeds like himself, but all of them resembled single species so closely it would take a detailed medical analysis to tell they were from Kayarsit.

He'd seen to it that they had the funds to join the most elite social circles, and they had almost finished infecting the planetary and financial leaders with the bacteria they had developed on their home planet.

But to keep the planetary leaders under control, Fellerd had to get the ingredients for the iocineil to the mixing lab. The bacterial retardant was the only thing that would keep them obedient to his orders. He had to have those fifteen planets. Once he was confident he could manage them, he could bring out his people from Kayarsit-III.

They'd follow his lead, and he would have Agnar-Alpha within a year. The space government of Vladmn, most planets, even the Amal, were unstable because every individual wanted to be at the top. They all wanted the power.

The Kayarsits were different. They would follow him because he knew more about the galaxy. Later they might need a new leader, but when that time came, he wouldn't object. The goal was to get his people out in the world where they would find enough food to reproduce to their maximum capabilities. In two years they would control the territory of Vladmn.

Only these single-species fools had to follow orders!

"It was the Olynthr who wanted me to use Hayden Haulers. . . ."

"Hayden Haulers?" Onetelles gave Fellerd his complete attention again. "The CD-51 the Halmarins captured was flying for Hayden Haulers?" He swallowed twice to keep his saliva from drooling down his chin.

"It isn't possible to know all the different hauling companies and the Olynthr said Quinta Norden was a friend of the owner. He thought it might help him. . . ."

"And they're planet hopping, asking questions?" Onetelles was more interested than ever.

"Even some of the Vladmn Patrol," Fellerd said, taking a step backward. "Not the whole patrol," he added, trying to save himself from being destroyed right there. "I've heard it was some friend of Captain Hayden's."

"Avvin?" Onetelles hissed out the name, removing his feet from the chair and rising in one lightning move.

"A Major Avvin." Fellerd took another step back.

"Relax," Onetelles snapped at the frightened cleosar. "You've done good work, if you've brought that group out here."

Onetelles had chaffed at not being able to hunt down Avvin and the pilot of that CD-51 that had taken the two escaping quinta from in front of him, making him look like a fool. He had waited, one reason for his impatience to bring about his plan was to gain the freedom to go back to Agnar-Alpha and get them.

Now the fool Fellerd had brought them out to him. It would be worth a dozen lost shipments to catch Avvin and the Icor girl away from their home planets.

"Get back to Agnar-Alpha and do the best you can with this mess," he ordered. "Get a new batch of berecine on its way."

While the cleosar hurried away across the crowded recreation area, Onetelles ambled in the other direction, keeping his movements carefully slow and blurred, indecisive, humanlike. His ship was waiting at the port. He could be off planet in an hour.

He stopped and looked back. He'd been wrong to send Fellerd away too quickly. He wanted all the information he could get on Avvin and Gella Icor. He turned and hurried after the cleosar, knowing he would frighten the fool into a stuttering incoherency, but that would be enjoyable, if indigestible.

To get the major and the female, he needed an information

network and a contact point to tell him where they were day by day. Fellerd, who could move around more freely, could set it up for him.

When he caught the nephew of the quinta and the dead smuggler's daughter he wasn't going to kill them outright. They deserved to be eaten alive.

CHAPTER 20

Neither Andro or Gella had been upset by Sis-Silsis's abruptness when they boarded *Destria*. Once their nearly mind-numbing relief had worn off, they both noticed the dullness of his golden scales, and the disproportionate number of slithers in the cockpit.

Sis-Silsis kept his hands on the controls of the ship, and his part of the conversation had been disjointed, delivered when he could take time from his adjustments.

"You're exhausted, and your nursery is hungry," Gella said. "Let me take over the controls for a little bit."

When Sis-Silsis relinquished the ship to her and left the cockpit, his offspring hastily followed. Andro, who had been with Conek when he first found the large droids and had worked with them more than Gella, was able to get through to Hercules. By trial and error he was able to get the big droid out of the copilot's seat and up against the rear bulkhead, where he could be strapped down and protected until he could be repaired.

Then Andro dropped into the vacant seat and stared out the right view port. Through the blowing dust he could occasionally catch a glimpse of the big black ship.

"You might try your luck with Deso," Gella suggested, nodding at the comm-unit.

Andro shook his head. "I've never had any luck with that ego-mechanical." He tried, but without result. When he couldn't raise Deso he tried Drumps. He didn't expect any success there. If Drumps was aboard and able to fly he would have taken over.

They were still discussing the problem when Sis-Silsis came back to the cockpit. Some of the gleam had returned to his scales. He was alone, which meant his numerous offspring were in the lounge, gorging themselves.

"How much control do you have over those hoppers?" he asked and shrugged when neither Gella nor Andro answered.

"There may be a way to get on board *Windsong*, but it's tricky." He reached over to flip open a small hidden plate on the control panel and took out an eight-centimeter-long plastene strip—an electronic key. "Not sure it will work in this magnetic soup."

"I don't understand," Andro complained.

"One of Conek's better ideas," Gella said. "Every ship in his fleet has an emergency lock, opened with a key like this one and a code. All his pilots know the code."

"Never thought we'd use it," the cynbeth said, looking at the key as if it were something alien and wonderful. "I always figured a problem serious enough to need the key would cause a crash."

"There's a small emergency air lock under *Windsong*. . . ." Gella said.

"Under?" Andro shook his head. "That would take some doing."

"It's the only way in," Gella said. "Someone has to be able to handle a hopper and keep it close enough for me to punch in the code, insert the key, and climb in."

"You're the best one to fly the hopper," Andro objected. "I'll do the stunt work."

"But you can't fly the ship," Gella reminded him.

"I'm supposed to fly under that wallowing monstrosity and keep a hopper within two meters of a hatch while you open it and climb in?" Andro shook his head. What was it about these people Conek hired that made them as crazy in their way as the Halmarins?

"If you can't do it, I will," Sis-Silsis snapped. "I brought Deso here. I'll see to it he gets Hayden's ship out."

"You stay aboard *Destria*," Gella said. "Major Avvin will fly the hopper and I'll do the acrobatics. I'd hate to see that ship crash, but I certainly don't want it to fall on that city below."

"Those people tried to kill you," the cynbeth said, looking at her curiously.

"I didn't escape," Gella said. "The guards let me go when the panic started." She looked as if she was ready to say more on the same subject, but instead she suggested she and Andro return to the rear hold and the hoppers.

Since the slithers were gathered around their feeders, they had no trouble in getting through the lounge. They were crossing the forward hold when Andro brought up the subject of her aborted remarks.

"I couldn't tell Sis-Silsis after what he's been through, but if none of you had come, I would have been off the planet by tomorrow night," Gella said.

"How?"

"Not all the Halmarins believe in the old customs. The fanatics are in power, but they're a minority. The others have an escape network for their people who can't or don't follow the old ways. I was going out that way. They were even going to let me take little Red."

"Then we've all risked our lives for nothing," Andro said bitterly.

"*I* don't think so." Gella smiled. "It makes me feel good to know so many people care."

"The next time I'll send you a Carlin Sun blossom," Andro groused.

"Thanks, but you see why I don't want to see their city destroyed?" Gella asked.

"Oh, yes, dearie, we do seem to always be out to save someone," Andro sighed as they closed the bulkhead hatch on the third hold and opened the wide deck doors. He climbed into the hopper Gella had flown because it appeared to have the strongest engine.

"Off we go to do our duty for Vladmn and all its dependent worlds," he muttered as he dipped through the grav opening and into the dust cloud.

Two minutes later he was under *Windsong*, hovering as Gella searched for the emergency hatch. He hoped she would find it soon. The Halmarins had made the connection between the stolen hoppers and the two ships hovering over the city before he had even known about *Destria*. Since they had not been spotted when they had entered the Osalt freighter, the Halmarins could still be searching for them.

A flash of fire burning through the dust cloud below told him he was right.

Gella, sitting beside him, looked down at the disappearing flash and turned back to scan the bottom of the ship. Two more streams of fire passed beneath them, but she ignored them. She pointed to a small bulge on the bottom of the ship and Andro maneuvered cautiously, bringing the hopper up so she could stand on the seat and reach the flat black surface.

Gella wasn't too worried about the shooting. The Halmarins were firing wide, they wouldn't risk hitting *Windsong*. They didn't want that giant ship to crash into their city. Still there might be some true fanatic up there who would see the death of hundreds of thousands as a way of protecting their souls.

As she stood up on the seat of the open hopper, she glanced down at Andro, more worried about him than the shooting. She'd shared enough dangers with him to know he wasn't a coward, but he was exactly what he called himself in times of stress; a button pusher. He'd do his best, but if he got rattled he might leave her hanging on a sky hook, not the most secure of positions.

There was the bulge. Just on the other side should be the handle and the lock that would give her entry into the alien ship. She motioned for Andro to slow down. The wind, combined with the roar of *Windsong*'s thrusters and the hopper's engines, made speech impossible. She wiggled her hand slightly to indicate he was to hover.

They'd discussed it all before they left Sis-Silsis on *Destria*, but she was going to be standing out there and she wanted to be sure he understood. Making an unexpected reappearance back in the detention cells through the roof would make her escape pointless. That was no way to teach these fanatics anything.

Above them, *Windsong* yawed and rolled. The handle that Gella had been reaching for rose five meters and slewed off more than fifteen to the right. She grabbed the top of the windscreen as Andro turned the ship and followed.

The wind that had been blowing at an even force for the past ten minutes started gusting. A cloud of brown dust roiled up around them, hiding the front end of the hopper from her sight. She dropped down into the seat. Getting scraped off if Andro came up too close under the black ship wouldn't get the job done.

At least the Halmarins couldn't see to shoot.

Then the dust darkened and Andro pointed up. Gella gave him the okay sign and stood up. He had either been lucky, or he was a precision pilot with a hopper. The bulge was right above her.

She stood up and felt for the handle. There it was, just where Conek had insisted it had to go. All the ships that flew for him had a uniform emergency entrance configuration.

"You forgot to give it a self-cleaner, boss," she muttered as she took an insecure grip with her left hand while with her right she attempted to wipe away the accumulation of grit from the windstorm.

Below her the dust cloud lightened and then she heard the explosion, felt the heat.

The hopper rose sharply for a few centimeters and then fell away below her. She clung to the anchoring handle, her feet dangling down in the billowing dust cloud. Her left hand was her only hold, and since her fingers gripped more grit than metal, she felt them slipping.

CHAPTER 21

Gella clung to the handle, her legs dangling down into the dust cloud. Somewhere below, between one and two hundred meters, were the tops of the buildings of the capital city of Halmarin-IV.

She should have worried more about Andro, she decided. She had been concerned that he might panic or lose his grip on logic with shots being fired at him. She should have worried more about his life.

She waited, dreading the sound of his crash, but when it didn't come she wasn't reassured. The roar of the thrusters on *Windsong* and the howl of the wind could have covered the noise if he had spiraled off and come down a kilometer or so away. The entire hopper hadn't exploded when it was hit, or she would have been blown off her precarious hold.

And she had to give some thought to her own position.

The fingers of her left hand were slipping on the grit caked on the small curved bar handle that gave her her only support until she could insert the plascard key. It would activate the cover over the code lock if the dust hadn't jammed it. Then she still had to punch in the code to open the hatch.

She wasn't going to make it.

She wasn't going to make it with the plascard in her right

hand, she amended, not yet willing to give up hope. She shoved the card back into the open pocket of her tunic and made a grab at the handle with her right hand.

She missed. The effort had caused her body to swing, and the gusting wind was pulling at her.

Don't look down, she warned herself, and then wondered why. She wouldn't be able to see anything but dust.

"Just don't look down," she muttered between clenched teeth and tried again. If she could just stop swinging. If the roaring of the engines would just stop.

"No, not stop," she said aloud, an attempt to negate that last thought. It would be bad enough to fall, but to have the ship fall on her—hell, what would be the difference? She wouldn't know it anyway.

She made another grab at the handle with her right hand, but the muscles in her left arm and shoulder were too tired to contract enough to raise her high enough to grasp it.

This is it, she thought, and fought the thought. She'd get up here, she had to. She tried again, but her arm was losing strength. It felt as if it were being pulled out of the socket.

She was willing herself to make one more try when she felt solidity under her feet. She looked down to see the nose of the hopper and felt the shudder of its vibrations though the swirling dust hid most of the little ship, but she could just make out the jagged hole in the port wing.

Andro was dividing his attention between trying to control the damaged hopper and trying to judge her position. He glanced up but made no effort to speak.

"Am I glad you happened to drop by," she muttered, knowing he couldn't hear her. The way the planetary airship was shaking he wouldn't be able to stay long.

She sighed for her aching left arm and looped it through the anchor handle. She should be okay. She raised her feet and motioned him away.

He shook his head, but she had braced her feet against a series of bolts on the bulge that protected the emergency hatch.

She waved him away again, and reached for the plascard key. It grated as it slid into the slot.

Nothing.

"Don't do this to me," she demanded. Below, the hopper had increased its vibrating. Andro made an abortive move to fly away and then seemed to think better of it. He tried to bring the hopper in close again, but he was losing what close control he had.

Gella hammered on the hand-sized panel that should have slid back to allow her to punch in the code. The third time she slammed her hand against it, it opened.

Now what was the code? If her left arm hadn't been hurting so she would have remembered.

Think, you idiot! Your only chance is up!

Parts of Conek's name. Something each of his pilots could associate with. Backward. K, E, N, `E—*Oh, my arm hurts!*—D.

The emergency hatch slid back. Gella caught onto the lip of the door with her right hand and swung one leg in.

She looked over her shoulder to see Andro release a hand from the controls long enough to give her a congratulatory sign. He should not have let go. The hopper dipped and as it fell out of sight, she saw the vibrating increase.

"Get back to *Destria*," she shouted after him, knowing he couldn't hear her.

Then she turned her attention back to getting aboard *Windsong*. She had both feet inside the ship when she discovered her problem. Her left arm had quit hurting. She couldn't feel it at all.

She also couldn't move it.

"This is no way to go through life," she muttered.

"What do you think you're doing?" shouted a voice from inside the ship.

Gella looked up to see Madder Drumps frowning down at her. His long, angular face was pale and his red hair stuck out in clumps on his narrow head—he had been pulling at it—a habit of his when concentrating. He looked decidedly unhappy, but at the moment Gella wasn't interested in his attitude.

"Help me in!" she shouted when he just stood staring.

"I really cannot have these interruptions in my work," the

scientist/pilot complained, apparently oblivious to her position.

"Then help me in," Gella yelled.

It took some shouted explanations before he understood he was to take a firm grip on her legs while she freed her numb arm, but when she finally convinced him it was either help her or put up with the possible added inconvenience of the ship crashing, he gave her a hand. Two, and surprisingly strong.

When Gella was aboard and they closed the hatch, he unstrapped a small pressurized atmospheric container that he used in his work and followed her to the main passage of the huge ship, complaining all the way.

"I want you to understand, I never interfere with the running of the ship, that is not a part of my private agreement with Captain Hayden," Madder continued to gripe as he ambled along in his loose-jointed walk. "But when we return to Agnar-Alpha I must complain about this rough flying and the interference to my equipment. It's been going on for hours, and my patience is wearing thin. If it doesn't stop soon, I intend to go forward and speak to Deso about it."

"You do that," Gella said. She would have liked to say more, which would include something about his duties as *Windsong*'s registered pilot, but he had come to his laboratory. The door closed behind him with a snap.

CHAPTER 22

Conek watched through the view ports of the cockpit as *Anubis* and Ister's Orelian Lapper landed. He had been monitoring the planet's spaceport transmissions and knew Sis-Silsis in *Destria*, Deso in *Windsong*, and Andro in his CC-12 were all in a landing pattern over Franklin.

"I still don't understand how they knew we were here," Quinta Norden said as she watched the Lapper land close to Skielth's Shashar Streamer. She wasn't objecting.

"They might not," Conek said, keying the switch to speak to the port authorities. He put in a request to have the three approaching ships assigned to pads close to his own.

"I made up a list of converging points in each sector for transferring cargo, or whatever we might need them for," Conek explained. He saw the sudden flicker in her eyes.

"I made the damn list five years ago," he snapped. Half his irritation was caused by her doubt. She seemed to be thinking he had been doing more shipping in the FarArm than he had said. Part of his anger came from admitting that in making his plans years before he had begun his company, he had spent a lot of time planning, hoping, and just plain dreaming.

He'd chosen Franklin because it had the reputation of being

the most respectable planet in the area. The spaceport was weedy, the buildings old and as in need of resurfacing as the pavement, but the port authority was reasonably efficient and as honest as could be expected on a backwater planet. Franklin had a small inter-system military patrol that kept away space pirates. Years ago when he chose it as an emergency meeting spot for his ships in the area, he hadn't expected to use it, and definitely not with a quinta on board.

Ister and Lesson had just reached the lounge on *Bucephalus* when the other three ships came in sight and maneuvered for landing positions. By common consent they waited until the others had shut down their engines and had left their ships. Conek was finding the liquors for Skielth to make Shashar bolts while the quinta reported on the arrivals from the cockpit.

"There's Andro getting out of that CC-12," she called out so she could be heard in the lounge. "Don't give him a bolt, or he won't be able to fly for a full day."

"If he wants one, *I'm* not telling him he can't have it," Skielth muttered. "She may run the government, but he runs the spaceport."

"There's a small red cynbeth on Sis-Silsis's back," she reported. "Who are those others—a rrotta and two mentots? They got out of *Destria*, but they've gone over to join Andro. Who is that with Deso and Madder Drumps—*it's GELLA!*"

In seconds they were all crowded in the cockpit to see for themselves. They stared out the view ports for nearly a minute before Ister voiced the first complaint.

"H-hayden!" he hissed. "You are s-standing on my tail!"

"Skielth is standing on your tail. My foot just happens to be sandwiched in there somewhere."

"I'd move, but Lesson's elbow is stuck in my armpit," the Shashar said.

"There's nothing I can do with these metal monsters crowded in behind me," Lesson grumbled.

"Everybody back into the lounge," Conek called out. "One at a time before someone gets trampled."

By the time they had sorted themselves out, the lounge elevator came up and Madder Drumps, Andro, and Gella stepped off first, with the two mentots. While the others made a fuss over Gella, and the scientist/pilot registered his complaint with Conek as though nothing in the tri-galactic territory mattered but his experiments, Andro sent the platform back down to bring up Lovey-I, Hercules, Deso, Sis-Silsis, and the rrotta.

Sleepy, Lovey-II, and Cge added to the confusion by enthusiastically greeting their fellow droids in Skooler whistles.

By the time the ten sentients and six droids were together in the lounge, the noise was deafening. Conek gave a shout to quiet the noise and suggested everyone fill their mouths with Skielth's Shashar bolts.

It worked for everyone except the droids. When Cge insisted on asking piping questions to his fellow mechanicals about their abilities to function and their need for service, Conek sent five of them into the forward hold. He ordered Deso to remain.

"First, I want to know how you got Gella out."

"Barely." Andro laughed and told them about her assistance from the Halmarin guards. "They had mapped out a path for her, only we had blocked it."

Fsith crouched down as Andro described the stench of the legords.

"The problem was getting back to the CC and getting it out," Sis-Silsis said. "I thought we'd never find that abandoned space hangar, but Major Avvin insisted. Couldn't leave Lovey-I, or you'd strangle him."

"No point in rewarding the Halmarins with one of my droids," Conek said, not willing to admit to them how angry he would be if he had lost one of the big devils. He'd never hear the end of it from Cge.

"Getting Gella was our prime concern, but now we've got to find her ship and find it fast."

"Oh, we'll find it," Sis-Silsis said, sitting back on his tail and admiring his drink before sticking his long tongue in it.

"We'll find it soon or not at all," Conek said, bringing everyone to attention. He told them what was in the cargo.

"I trust there will be none of that aboard *Windsong*," Madder Drumps said, looking at Deso uneasily.

"That *dirty*—" Gella came up out off her lounger, her eyes flashing. "I'll *kill* that . . ."

"Vladmn will do it for you," Norden snapped. "There's a death penalty waiting for him. Humans learned their lessons about addictives and hallucinogenics back in pre-space times. At first they allowed their pseudo-intellectuals to preach tolerance. Their judges talked about it as a victimless crime, and some believed it until the public discovered those judges were in the pay of the criminals."

"Anyone who'd say anything that dumb had to be," Skielth said.

"They had to enact capital punishment and enforce it before they cleaned up their society," Norden said. "We don't repeat the mistake of leniency to addicters."

"If you get him first, you can have him," Gella answered, not ready to give up her revenge.

"You'll let him alone, love." Andro smiled at her with irritating sweetness. "You and Conek need his trial to prove you weren't a part of it."

"We won't have him or the ship if we don't get at it," Conek snapped. "How's that magnetic storm doing?"

"It's healthy as all hell," Lesson replied as he took a sip of his bolt. Conek didn't care much for the look of pleasure the old pilot showed. This was no time for Lesson to take one of his spirituous downtimes.

"It's moving in like it planned a long visit," Sis-Silsis said as he pulled Risee's head out of his glass. "Let you get started on these things, and the others will want them too," he told the slither. The cynbeth loved the taste of liquor, but no intoxicant, addictive, or hallucinogen known affected their systems.

"I wonder. If the magnetics are strong enough, what effect they could have on the atmospheric mix," Drumps said dreamily. "If you are going to search those areas anyway, I would like to send trap cannisters with you. Even if I could detect some temporary changes . . ."

"Love, you're not quite into the spirit of the emergency," Andro said.

"Pilot Drumps, this is not a scientific expedition for your

benefit." Norden jumped up and paced the room, frowning at the assembly.

Conek knew she was starting in on a tirade, but she wasn't able to get started before the alarm rang on the lounge lift, and after Ister freed the release, Olvar entered the lounge. He was a tall, lanky human who flew Conek's fifth ship, *Traveler*. He had been making a series of routine but profitable runs between two planets on the far side of Beta Galaxy.

Conek's other pilots called him Chatterbox, with reason. Olvar had obviously heard of Gella's arrest by the Halmarins and had come to help. He explained with his customary loquacity.

"She's out."

The rest of the group had questions for Olvar, most of which he answered with slow looks under lowered eyebrows, but they were interrupted by Norden who demanded the floor again.

"If you refuse to take this problem seriously, I'll call in the Vladmn Patrol."

"That means arrest for Conek, Gella, and maybe the others," Andro warned her. "And by the time you can get through a PME to have the patrol search, it could be too late."

"You'd have better luck curling your hair with a blaster." Conek didn't need to remind her of the last time the Planetary Military Emergency law had been put in force. The Vladmn Council had enacted it when the Amal was in power and it had put every planet in the territory in jeopardy.

But Norden didn't make idle threats. If she said she was willing to try, then she'd do it. That was the hell of working with a quinta. They could *do* things.

"Let's show the quinta what good little kids we can be when we want to," Conek urged, not wanting to wait out the rest of his life on Balazaro while his friends tried to prove he wasn't smuggling addictives, since iocineil had been classified as one. "Let's give nice little reports on what happened and see what we've learned. I'll start and show you how to share."

By the time Conek had told his story of his trip to Orser, Skielth, Lesson, and the others had added their tales, a pattern had emerged. Nelsf, curled affectionately around his glass, looked up, his eyes unfocused and wandering.

"I don't think they like strangers," he said after listening to all the stories of being attacked, ambushed, mugged, and followed.

"And most of the planetary authorities don't love us much either," Lesson said. "All these questions are like poking sticks in dark holes. We've stirred up the local wrong-side runners. Most of them think we've been brought in by their competitors."

"Competitors?" Norden asked.

"They're mostly organized in small groups," Ister said. "Each one is trying to get the business of the ones on the next planet over."

"Seems each little group thinks we've been hired as the big guns to get rid of them. No convincing them we don't care what they do."

"How did you find this out?" Andro asked.

"Got half arrested," Lesson snapped, not happy to admit he had not outrun the Vergal patrol ships. "We traded a little talk after they searched our ships and they decided we weren't in with their local wrong-side runners. Lucky they don't like the Halmarins. Gave us the benefit of the doubt.

"We stirred up a bunch on Laver, but they were already busy blasting away at another group and had got the local law on their tails. Seems there's about six small organizations out there that think we're working for their competitors. We've started two or three little wars."

"If they destroy each other they'll save Vladmn the trouble," Norden said crisply.

"But, that's not the point," Ister said softly. "They all think we're working for their competitors, so they'll all be after us."

CHAPTER 23

"This is a mess! A real mess!" Conek paced up and down the lounge of *Bucephalus* while Quinta Norden sat on one of the reclining seats and watched him. He turned around and glared at her. When she showed no response he pointed his finger.

"No disrespect intended, your greatness, but you'll prevent me from finding that berecine."

"Don't be ridiculous. Sit down and eat your food before it gets cold. Lovey-II, get the captain a cup of feine."

"I don't need anyone to tell me what to eat or drink or when," Conek stormed at her. "How can I go where I need to go with you aboard?"

"Are you suggesting the ship won't be able to carry my additional weight, Captain?"

By the passage that led to the cabins and the food preparation compartment, Lovey-II rolled uneasily back and forth. He was caught between the quinta's order for him to bring feine for the captain and his apparent rejection of it. Seeing the droid's confusion gave Conek another reason for griping.

"And you're confusing my mechanicals! Go get the feine, Two." At least he had convinced Lovey-I and Lovey-II to answer to a numeral. Then he remembered his gripe at the quinta.

"You didn't have to come. Andro could have taken you and Gella back to Agnar-Alpha. You'd be safely out of it by now!"

"And half the Vladmn Patrol would be shooting at you," she snapped back, tiring of his complaints.

"More important, you would have lost your chance to keep an eye on me, right?"

"Sometimes I need to!" she shouted back. Then her expression changed from anger to a straightforward speculation. "But it may surprise you to know I believe you have the best chance of finding that ship and that explosive."

Faith, from Norden. He didn't believe it for a minute.

"Why? Do you think I know something I haven't told you?"

"No," Norden spoke slowly, for once sounding unsure of herself. "I don't know—perhaps it's some sort of primeval shrewdness, the ability to make quantum jumps in logic, or just blind luck—but for some reason you accomplish what you set out to do. I think you'll find it if anyone will."

"And if I find it but not in time? That stuff has a reputation of going off unexpectedly."

"I promise I won't file a complaint." She picked up the steaming tray of food and started to eat as if she were hostessing a formal dinner.

Conek swore under his breath and picked at his food with a tyne. His mind was too full of irritations to worry about his stomach.

Having the quinta on board *Bucephalus* put a severe limitation on him. He tried to tell himself she asked for any trouble they ran into, but he couldn't buy it. It was his opinion that Norden didn't recognize or admit her own importance. After Bentian's resignation she was the senior quinta of Vladmn. Her will was stronger than the other four who were hardly more than puppets of their coalitions, and her ability to bully them made her, within certain limitations, the ruler of the Vladmn Federation.

Moreover, she was one politician Conek trusted. She was bossy, irritating, damned infuriating, but when Vladmn needed her, she was there. Only she wouldn't be if she was on *Bucephalus* at just the wrong time.

"You didn't have to stay," Conek muttered, his mouth full of roast Canerian waterfowl. The dish was a delicacy and he usually saved it for times when he had the leisure to fully enjoy it. Right then the taste was lost under his frustrations.

"When you sent word about the base on Vilarona, you could have left. The patrol probably wouldn't have come after me once they had your story."

"Once they heard me out, they would have rescinded the arrest order," she agreed, nodding enthusiastically. There was a catch to her admission, Conek decided. He waited.

"But in this magnetic storm, what would be the chances of the patrol ships getting the message?"

Conek gave her a wolf grin. This time she had slipped up. Her logic wasn't foolproof.

"The ones that didn't get the message wouldn't have known you'd left the ship," Conek said. Damn, why hadn't he thought of that before they left Franklin? Across the room, Norden's eyes widened. It gave him some small satisfaction to know she hadn't thought of it either.

"It's too late to argue about that now," she said, dismissing the remark as unimportant. "And if I'm not mistaken . . ."

She wasn't. The alarm was sounding. They'd be coming out of time in twenty minutes. He had deliberately set the alarm to sound early so he had time to strap the droids in the hold and shut them down before the magnetic interference caused them to glitch. A group of mechanicals running amuck was the last thing he needed.

Norden rose and hurried toward the food preparation center, carrying her empty dish.

"I'll see to the computers," she said, knowing what Conek had planned with the droids. While he was busy with them she would return to the cockpit and dump the data into a heavily shielded storage data holder Conek had bought on Franklin.

Conek called to the droids to follow him into the forward

hold behind the passenger staterooms. He had strapped Lovey-II in place when he realized Cge wasn't giving out with his usual orders.

"Where's that damned Cge?" he grumbled, looking back toward the hatch. He hadn't seen his smallest mechanical since he had sent the droids back to have their own gossip session on Franklin. He'd been too busy arguing with Norden to notice.

"He left the ship with Lovey-I," Lovey-II informed him. "He communicated to me his need to assist PilotGellaIcor."

"And you didn't tell me?" He glowered at the big unit whose sensor lights slowed, trying to work out the problem.

"Is it a part of my programming that I should tell you when another unit leaves the ship?" Lovey-II asked.

"Damn right, if I don't want them to go!"

"Cge was not to leave the ship," the big droid said slowly. "How was I . . . ?"

"Just shut up and shut down!" Conek griped as he re-checked the straps. When he looked up again, the droid's panel was dark.

He didn't have to worry about Norden and the magnetic storms glitching his units; he could manage that himself, he decided as he started back toward the cockpit. He wondered if he should have reactivated Lovey-II and explained. But how the hell did you explain anger to a robot?

And what glitch in that stupid little unit made him decide to go off with Gella?

"I hope to hell they have enough people on that CC," Conek griped when he told Norden what he had learned. Andro had left in his borrowed vessel, taking Lovey-I and Gella with him. Knowing his little droid, he was reasonably sure Cge would stay hidden until he decided he was needed. They wouldn't know to shut him down.

Cge might get his final glitch.

While he waited for the gray of time-comp to dissolve into the black of normal space, Conek set up a coded message to send when he returned to normal space. He hoped Andro would pick it up and find Cge before he permanently glitched himself. There was very little hope Andro would hear it.

They came out of time over the Halmarin system. Conek raised the visual view ports and nodded. The scene was what he had expected. The magnetic storm had had little effect on their reentry into normal space, so they were hanging just off Sextus, the sixth planet in the system. They were a little closer in than Conek had expected to be. He was glad he had given himself a wide margin of safety.

The Halmarins had hidden *Starfire*, why, Conek wasn't sure. Perhaps Norden was right in thinking they might suspect Gella's friends of trying to steal the ship and rig the computer information to prove Icor's innocence. They could have expected to find some sort of contraband on board that would prove the daughter, like the father, was a hardened criminal.

He discounted Sis-Silsis's suggestion that they would keep the ship, camouflage it, and add it to their fleet as their own. The Halmarins were religious fanatics, not thieves.

He didn't believe they had taken it to Halmarin-IV. That would have been too obvious. They would not have taken it out of their system. That would have been stupid.

The Halmarin system had nine planets, five of them at least partially habitable, making it the most life-supporting star in the three galaxies. It was rare that a star had one habitable planet, and rarer still for there to be more than one.

Most were only partially habitable, even with underground colonies. On Sextus, the sixth and coldest, only the equator was warm enough to allow mining.

At their meeting on Franklin, they had agreed that *Starfire* would not be on Neocar, since a Vladmn Patrol officer had witnessed the ship's departure from that planet.

That still left four planets, since he could be wrong and it could be on the capital world.

"And Gella wasn't sure about the distress signal?" Norden asked, though Conek had answered the question before. The repetition of the question soothed his irritation at her. It was a sign of stress. He didn't want her flipping out on him, but her poise sometimes made him feel he was the only one who could get a little shaky at times.

Conek had added a safety feature to all the ships flying for him. They carried a timed distress signal that he had ordered turned on before they left the ship on any port other than Agnar-Alpha. If they did not turn it off within one standard day, it would start sending. Only Gella had not planned on leaving the ship. She couldn't remember whether or not she had turned it on or not. If she had, it might not be strong enough to override the magnetic interference.

While his computers went wild in the magnetic storm, Conek manually flew in the direction of the terminator line. They would do their searching on the dark side of the planet, out of the direct path of the magnetic disturbances.

Using the planet as a shield helped, but Secundus seemed to have some sort of interference of its own. Instead of having all the ship's sensors on one hundred percent wild, they were able to use them at least one minute out of every five.

"The whole idea is impossible!" Norden said as she cleared a short-range heat sensor and turned it on again. "We're never going to find that ship under these conditions."

"If you've got a better idea, let's hear it," Conek said, trying to keep the ship stable with one hand while he flipped switches to clear the overload on the long-range screens.

"Here's something," Norden said. "Could be static, but I think I saw the outline of a vessel."

"We'll go down." Conek left the long-range scanners to go wild while he brought the ship down closer to the surface. He didn't hold out much hope, but they were over a hilly, rocky area where a ship might be hidden.

"It was probably just stat—" Norden paused and lowered the hand-held distance viewer to glance at Conek. "That is definitely a ship under that overhang. It could be a freighter —CD size."

"I'll make another pass," Conek said. He cursed his luck at having the quinta with him. If he were alone, he could land and check it out.

She didn't see herself as an obstacle to reconnaissance and made the suggestion herself. Ten minutes later, all his arguing and swearing was still falling on deaf ears. She ordered him to land.

"But you'll stay aboard, and if I'm not back in an hour, you get out of here," he said as he shut down the thrusters and left the cockpit, not that it would do a bit of good.

"I'm coming with you," Norden replied as she followed him back to his sleeping compartment and watched him strap on his blaster belt. He hated it when she ignored his bad temper and answered so sweetly.

"If that is *Starfire*, you'll need help." She reached into the cabinet and pulled out his second blaster holster belt and tried to buckle it. It would have fallen to the floor if she hadn't caught it.

"They must have loaded a nullifier with the berecine. You'll need me to help you deactivate it."

"That's what I don't understand," Conek griped. "If they were going to use a neutralizer anyway, then why not put it in before they shipped it?"

"Because the chemical makeup of berecine keeps it changing," Norden said. "It's never stable. They have to make their final mixture within hours of giving it to the io-heads, or it loses its affect." She read his irritation that he hadn't known about it.

"I read up on it while you were installing the new shielded data storage."

"There's one problem with this idea," Conek said, going back to his original complaint. "There's a lot of things I can do, but I'm not a good sneaker-upper-in-the-dark. I've tried it a few times, and it's never worked. I don't think you should be along."

"In that case I'm certainly going," Norden said as she punched an additional hole in the belt. "You need my political expertise." She gave him an impish grin. "I'm in a sneaky business."

"You stay behind me," he muttered as he led the way through a dense undergrowth that felt warm to the touch, damp and soft, and gave him the uneasy feeling that it was more life than plant, and possibly had a big appetite.

Damn, he hated wandering around strange places in the dark. With his luck they probably had unfriendly reptiles too.

He got along well with the sentient kind, but the non-sentients gave him the shivers.

Norden made a small sound and Conek turned in time to see her pull her hair away from one of the bushes. The thick, fingerlike branches, or branchlike fingers, were waving without any wind to stir them.

They moved farther away from the undergrowth and continued over the hill. They could see the gleam of metal from the shadows, but the undergrowth kept them from identifying the ship.

"We'll have to go all the way down," Norden whispered.

"I'll go down. You stay up here and cover me," Conek said, and wasn't surprised when she refused. He started to argue and then thought better of it. By the time he was finished, she would have decided to go alone and leave him on guard. Sometimes he didn't like the quinta much.

Conek led the way down the slope, staying as close to the swaying plants as he dared. He needed their shadow. He didn't need their interest in him.

He was within six meters of the ship before he was sure it was a CD-51.

It couldn't be *Starfire*. It couldn't be this easy, he thought and crept up closer. There were still plants between him and the vessel. Strange, they weren't swaying as the others were.

He stepped closer, touched one, and discovered it was hard and lifeless. It was also rootless and precariously balanced. When it fell a series of lights flared up, illuminating the entire area. Just to the side of the ship a light showed as a curtain was thrown back and three blurred shadows stepped out. Blinded by the light, Conek could only tell they stood upright, humans or humanoids, but he could see their arms, and even half blind he could recognize blasters when he saw them.

"Don't move," the first one ordered. He spoke Vladmn Standard with a human inflection. His accent was Alpha Galaxy FarArm.

"I can't see to go anywhere, so easy with that weapon,"

Conek replied, his hands still up over his eyes. He hoped Norden had escaped. She might have if she had been far enough behind him. The shock of the sudden light was still blinding him.

"Someone else here," the second one said. He sounded human, but as he stepped between Conek and one of the glaring lights his silhouette showed a spindly humanoid body and a large, misshapen head. An Emininian.

"It's a woman."

So much for getting the word out, Conek thought.

The human ordered them into the small cavern that had been hidden by the light-proof curtain. It was a single chamber cave, lit by a single illuminator, cold and damp. A cracked board lay across two rocks, a couple of boulders had been worked out of the earth and stone walls and had been rolled over to the board, presumably for seats. On the smoothest part of the floor three grav-sheets were piled with wrinkled coverings.

Not much of a hideout.

The Emininian stood guard while his human companion went back outside to turn off the lights and reset their makeshift alarm system.

When he came back in he stood over them, his blaster still in his hand. Conek eyed the old-style blaster and wondered if it would shoot. It looked like a relic from a museum. So did their clothing. If they were typical of FarArm smugglers, it would pay them to turn honest.

"Who are you?"

"Strangers, dropped in by mistake," Conek said. "Strictly the wrong address." He meant it. The illuminated glimpse he caught of the CD told him it wasn't *Starfire*.

"Think they're Halmarin law?" the second one asked.

"We're a little too tall, don't you think?" Conek asked in return.

"We have nothing to do with law or patrols and we don't want to," Norden spoke up, shaking out her hair that had been pulled out of its neat arrangement by the bush.

Conek watched with a slight frown as she moved slightly,

not enough to give them the idea she was trying to rise. She slowly eased into a blatantly seductive pose.

"I've just escaped from Halmarin-IV," she said, giving her voice a sultry purr. "We're looking for my ship. I'm Gella Icor. Maybe you've heard of my father?"

CHAPTER 24

Gella sat in the copilot's seat of the old CC-12 and watched Andro wrestle with the controls. Below them the cloud cover of Secundus was a fast swirling mass of pale gray clouds. There would be violent storms below, and not because of the magnetic storm. Secundus was a fast-moving, small planet that whirled about its sun sharing its orbit with a nearly identical twin, Rilvik, which always remained hidden on the other side of the star Halmarin.

"Oh, my nerves!" Andro gasped and swung away as *Windsong* came out of time. The giant black ship was less than its own length away from the small freighter and yawing dangerously.

"It wasn't Drumps's fault," Gella said, holding on to the arms of her seat even though she was securely strapped in. "You just don't know in this crazy storm."

"Tell me about it, love." Andro slowed after he maneuvered to a safe distance. "But it didn't seem to bother Olvar, there he is. I just hope it hasn't—it has, coming out too close has scrambled what serves Drumps for a mind."

The comm-unit speaker blared with static and Drumps's panic. The transmission was too broken for them to understand his words, but his fear was unmistakable.

"You should have flown that alien monstrosity," Andro griped, trying to reach the scientist pilot on the hand unit.

"He didn't trust me to do it," Gella reminded Andro.

"Conek should have ordered it, even if he had to take Drumps on *Bucephalus* with him."

"He didn't do it though, and the only thing you can do now is land and find out what his problem is," Gella said, stating the obvious.

She was treated to a lengthy and colorful list of smuggling curses that Andro had picked up from Conek before they reached the surface of the planet, but it wasn't long before Drumps had followed Andro down. *Traveler* was close behind and all three ships sat on the heat-fused surface of the small world of Secundus. Only the polar regions were partially habitable, and even then it would be fatal for most species to remain in the open too long. The Secundans lived in small colonies underground and tapped into the rock fissures to trap and condense gases that liquefied under cooler temperatures.

Exactly what they trapped was some sort of industrial secret. Gella had never been interested in finding out. Alpha's FarArm had never been her territory and if she ever got out of it, she never intended to come back.

If she ever got out of it.

She stayed in the cockpit and watched as Andro, in a heat protective suit, hurried across to the big black ship, Lovey-I at his heels. Since they had landed on the night side of the planet, and Lovey-I had been able to function again, Gella had talked Andro into putting the unit aboard his native ship. She didn't know if the alien skin of the ship would give the droid any added protection, but then Andro didn't either. Her reasons had sounded plausible, and he was an administrator, not a droid expert.

She waited until he had ridden the grav-beam up into the hold on *Windsong* and unstrapped her safety harness. On the dark side of the planet, the comm-links worked. As soon as she moved to the pilot's seat and revved the thrusters in preparation for takeoff, she heard Drumps's panicked voice.

"Major Avvin, I protest, you can't just leave me here."

"He won't, he's already aboard *Windsong*," Gella answered. "Give him a message for me. Tell him I know how to find out where they hid *Starfire*."

She switched off the communicator to prevent any further conversation and raised the ship, heading for Halmarin-IV.

When she had listened to Conek's plans for the search of the Halmarin system, she had become more and more convinced that her ship was on the capital planet. From the little she knew of berecine, it seemed to her that the temperature extremes on the others would have increased the instability of the berecine until it would have already exploded.

Some of the Halmarins were religious fanatics and distrustful of the motives of anyone who did not embrace their own particular faith, but they were good people. She had seen that when she had been their prisoner.

The rest of the universe might not agree with them, but they did live according to their beliefs. They didn't deserve what would happen to them if that terrible force on *Starfire* was to explode.

She set her jump coordinates carefully. She was only in time-comp a short time; Secundus and Halmarin-IV were in their closest proximity.

It was luck, an accident of timing rather than any planning on her part, that brought her out over the capital city at night when the communications were considerably clearer.

She asked for a direct channel to the Minister of Justice, Charno-vins. It wasn't long in answering.

"Why have you returned?" the minister asked.

"When your Colonel Hubrin confiscated my ship I was unaware that part of the cargo I carried . . ." She went through the long and involved explanation of how Hayden Haulers had been used to transport the berecine and the inevitable destruction that would occur if it was not located and neutralized.

"I'll surrender if you'll give me your word to let our people aboard the ship to mix the nullifier," she said. "You can have your people oversee the work. There won't be any tricks."

"And you are willing to surrender to your just punishment if I agree to this?" Charno-vins asked.

"I am. If you give me your word that you will allow them aboard the ship, I will immediately land and surrender."

"You have my word," the Minister of Justice answered slowly, as if he begrudged it.

Gella flipped off the communications switch and sighed. She too had given her word, and there was nothing for it but to land and give herself up. She could understand Charno-vins's reluctance, but he was submitting to the saving of his life. She might be giving hers up.

"There's no point in holding out much hope that Conek can find the other ship," she said. She said it aloud, trying to force herself to understand the risk so she wouldn't rail at fate later.

A few minutes later she set the CC-12 down on the landing pad of the main spaceport on Halmarin-IV. Outside the ship, hoppers buzzed around as if someone had turned over a hive of nectar sippers.

When she stepped out of the ship, Charno-vins hurried from one of the small surface skimmers, a blaster in his hand.

"I'm not armed," she said. "I told you I'd surrender if you'd tell us where my ship is and let them . . ."

"Your ship is where your people will not find it," Charno-vins cut her off.

"You gave your word," Gella said, not believing what she heard.

"The word of a Halmarin is sacred when speaking to a clean soul, but yours is stained with the deaths of our people. It would be a sacrilege to allow you to call on the honor of the faithful."

CHAPTER 25

Conek couldn't help but admire Norden's presence of mind when she had claimed to be Gella. It seemed to him a stroke of genius. In Alpha FarArm the contrabanders didn't stick up for each other like the ones who flew under Tsaral's loose organization, but if they believed her they would know she and Conek didn't mean them any harm.

At least that was his first thought.

It didn't last long as he watched the face of the largest of their captors. It slowly changed from pale to red and on to purple.

"Do I know Icor?" he thundered. "If I could get my fingers on his scrawny neck, I'd choke the life out of that old crook."

"My father . . ."

"Besides, now I look at you closer, you couldn't be his kid. You're too old—old enough to be her mother."

Conek tensed and got ready to move. No one, absolutely *no* one insulted a quinta. It wouldn't help a bit that they didn't know who she was. She'd been too powerful for too long to take it. He was right.

"I'm *what*?" Norden's eyes blazed, and in one instant swing of her arm, she had swept the illuminator off the table and had flung it at the man who had insulted her.

He had been taken off guard and ducked as he fired his blaster. The disintegrating fire cut the board of the table in half as Conek made a dive for the smaller man who blinked at the unexpected result of his companion's remark. Conek had the man's weapon before he could move.

"Hold it, friend," Conek said, keeping the large-headed Emininian between himself and the place where he had last seen the human before the light had crashed to the floor.

"I've found his gun," Norden called out in the darkness. "Let's get out of here."

Conek swore and pushed the humanoid away from him, ready to make a dash for the entrance, but Norden's shout had given the human the idea of escape, if he hadn't already had it. The light-proof curtain jerked aside and he was out of the entrance a few steps before Norden. Conek managed to catch up with her just before she dashed outside.

"Hold it," he muttered, pulling her back so hard she bumped into the wall. "You want to get cut in half?"

"He's unarmed," she jerked, trying to pull away.

"The other one isn't," he snapped. "There was a third one." He'd been too busy worrying about the ones he could see to remember there had been three figures in the doorway, but his well-honed sense of survival brought it back to mind.

As if to prove it, a flash of fire came through the curtain, burning a curved slash across the fabric. They pressed close to the wall while the sweeping fire cut swaths until the center section of the old cloth flopped down, leaving a meter-wide hole in their scanty protection.

"We could have made it outside," Norden said, her voice sharp.

"You could have waited before throwing your tantrum," Conek groused.

"I didn't see you doing anything spectacular!"

"No one accused me of being Gella's mother."

"Careful, Captain, or I might be leaving here by myself! Now do something!"

"Just what do you suggest?"

While he had been baiting the quinta, Conek had been thinking. Their first problem was not to get out, but to find out what the Emininian was up to. Conek had shoved him to the side when he made a dash to keep Norden from running out into waiting blaster fire. The humanoid could have another weapon back in the cave somewhere, and if so they could be caught in a cross fire.

"You slip up close to the curtain and look out," Norden was saying, taking command. "When you spot them, I'll give you fire cover while you get outside. Then we'll have them . . ."

Conek had been right, she was accustomed to giving orders, and she'd run things if she were given a chance, but he wasn't listening. While she was talking he was moving back into the cave, staying close to the wall. His foot touched the illuminator and he reached down to pick it up. He didn't attempt to use it. It would target them to the waiting smugglers outside.

Norden was still whispering when he saw the stealthy movement of a shadow silhouetted between himself and the torn curtain. The spindly humanoid was moving toward the entrance, some sort of long and probably heavy object held in both hands and raised above his head. It was hard to judge distance in the darkness, but he couldn't be very far from the quinta.

Conek made a dash for the Emininian. He closed with him just as the smuggler was swinging at Norden. Conek couldn't stop the blow; his only chance was to deflect it. He plowed into the humanoid with a force that carried them both beyond the quinta, into the curtain that tore away under their weight, and sent them sprawling on the rocky ground in front of the cave.

They rolled on the ground, caught up in the rags of the curtain, and knocked over one of the cut bushes that kept the alarm wire in place. The open area in front of the rock overhang was illuminated in glaring light again. Then a large hairy hand pulled away the fabric and Conek found himself looking up into the nozzle of the third smuggler's blaster. Behind it was the maned head of a talovan. Conek had seen that face before. It was easy to recognize since the mane on the left side of the talovan's head was singed.

"This is a strange place to find hermil," he griped as he relinquished the Emininian's blaster.

"And a stranger place to find you," the talovan retorted. "Going to tell me you're not after me this time?"

"I wish to hell that you'd take your CD somewhere so I didn't keep running into it," Conek said, rising. He was too angry to think the hermil smuggler from Orser would do him any harm.

"I'm in a hurry, I've got things to do, and you keep getting in my way!"

"Seems to me we came a long way and did a lot of hiding to get in your way," the talovan snarled.

"If you had any sense, you wouldn't be on any of the Halmarin planets right now," Conek told him about *Starfire* and what she carried.

"And believe me, we don't have time for this foolishness," Norden said from the entrance of the cave.

"Who is that?" the ragged human demanded.

"I am *not* Gella Icor's mother, and that's all you need to know," Norden snapped. "Now put away your weapon, or I'll really get angry."

"For space sake, don't make her any worse than she is," Conek said, grinning. "I've got enough trouble."

"You're not Vladmn Patrol?" the Emininian asked, getting to his feet. He had been slightly stunned by hitting the ground.

"I said no, and I'm tired of your paranoia."

"May be something to what they're saying," the human said, scratching his scraggly, unkempt hair. "Told you what I saw. Sounds like it could have been about the time the girl was grabbed, if his story is true."

"Keep talking," Conek ordered as if he were the one holding the blaster.

"Halmarin patrol ship, coming in with a CD-51 following it. They put the CD in a hangar at one of their abandoned spaceports up in the mountains above the city."

"On what planet?" Conek demanded.

"Halmarin-IV. I was with Rono—I was with a pal of mine and we had ducked over there to—well, never mind why."

Conek felt his little critter walking up his backbone again.

Damn! He had been sure they would not take the ship to the capital planet!

"How do we find it?"

"Well, it's best to go in over the ocean, follow the coastline down until you come to a jut of land that sticks out into the water and splits. Called the Forked Tongue, I think. Then you turn straight east—look for a pass in the mountains, and it's straight . . ."

"That's where Andro left the CC," Norden said, running across the flat open space from the cave entrance. In her excitement she had forgotten she was supposed to be holding the gun on the FarArm smugglers, maintaining their half of the standoff.

"He was sitting right on *top* of it," Conek said, thinking they didn't need any complications but their own stupidity and bad luck. If it had not been for the magnetic storm, the sensors on the old CC would have picked up the ship when he first landed.

"And that stuff is really aboard?" the talovan asked, still not quite convinced.

"It's there all right. If you want to risk your life to see the proof, come along."

"No, don't think I want to do that. Think we're in any danger here?"

"Not at the present, but if that stuff goes off I wouldn't build any permanent structures or found any dynasties in this system."

"And you're going after it?"

"That's the idea. Don't take offense if we don't stay to dinner."

The talovan holstered his weapon. "Come on then. We'll fire up and take you over to your ship."

"I don't know whether to thank you or not," Conek said. Their destination was more dangerous than a blaster.

CHAPTER 26

Sentients were illogical. Cge had tried to calculate their behavioral patterns, but he had not been at the task very long when he decided not even the largest and most advanced computers in Vladmn would be successful. He found the mobility of human faces fascinating to watch, and had worked out simple formulas for concluding the general trend of their planned actions.

When the pilots of the ships met on Franklin, and ConekHayden had sent the droids back into the forward hold, Cge had slipped into a stateroom and listened to the conversation through an open door. Later he had stood unnoticed in the passageway and watched his owner and his friends.

That was when he knew Gella Icor was making plans of her own. Her eyes were sad; Cge's owner had explained emotions to him, and Deso had told him sadness, worry, fear, and other hurting emotions were something like a minor malfunction in a droid.

There was a tightness around her mouth, the kind ConekHayden got when he had decided to do something and refused to be persuaded by his friends.

And she was quiet.

To Cge, those three factors summed up to mean she was

going to do something that she didn't want to do, and somehow she was going to do it without letting the others know until it was too late for them to stop her.

If they would have stopped her, then it was probably dangerous. He had been with ConekHayden long enough to understand danger and trouble.

Deciding what to do about what he knew took more calculations. He could tell ConekHayden—

Reject.

If Gella had decided to put herself in danger, she would find a way. He should protect her. That was what his owner would want, though if ConekHayden knew, he would not allow his smallest droid to even try. He would help his owner and protect Gella, but like her, he wouldn't tell anyone what he was planning.

He waited until QuintaNorden suggested that Gella fly with Androthemajor in his CC-12, and he hurried through the holds, activating the grav-rev beam in the fourth cargo area. He still didn't like to ride them, but this time he was glad his owner had made him learn.

It was easy to find a place to hide aboard the old freighter. It had belonged to a smuggler, and Cge's sensors soon found a hidden panel. The small recess behind it was just large enough if he crouched.

Luckily he was close enough to hear the conversation between Gella and Androthemajor, so he knew when they landed on Secundus and Gella left Androthemajor and Lovey-I to fly on *Windsong*, and when Gella reached Halmarin-IV.

He softly whistled his distress when he learned she was landing and surrendering herself to the Halmarins, but he knew that was what she had decided on board *Bucephalus*.

He would not be able to stop her, but he might rescue her as Androthemajor had done. His owner had been glad of that.

Illogical. He could not save her but he could rescue her? But was that less logical than Gella's escape only to return and surrender again?

He whistled his confusion as she left the ship after landing at the main Halmarin-IV spaceport.

As soon as she was off the CC-12, he scrambled out of

his hiding place and scurried to the cockpit, watching out the viewports. He saw the Halmarin surround her, some with blasters in their hands. He couldn't hear what was said, but he saw one dressed in bright green and orange shake his head. Gella tried to step back, as if she wanted to return to the ship.

They surrounded her and pushed her into a ground speeder. Before he could decide if there was anything he could do, the little vehicle had sped off down a dark street.

With no one to hear him, he gave full vent to whistling his frustration. The capital city was too large for him to search for her, and he had lost sight of the speeder.

He stopped his calculations as he saw four Halmarins coming his way. They were coming for the ship! When Gella had been captured the first time they took her ship, and they had planned to kill the little cynbeth when they executed her.

Would they deactivate him?

ConekHayden wouldn't like that at all.

The idea didn't fit well in his computer either.

He reached forward and flipped the switch that raised the ramp and closed the entrance hatch. He saw one of the Halmarins lift a hand communicator to speak, and Cge turned off the comm-unit before they could give him an order.

But what should he do next?

He couldn't allow himself to be taken and deactivated. He could not let them have Androthemajor's ship—

Androthemajor knew how to find the place where Gella would be taken.

But he was on Secundus.

Cge looked down at the flight controls. He had never been programmed as a pilot, but he had watched, and he had stored the data.

He pushed the button that brought the pilot's seat closer to the flight console, climbed up, strapped himself in, and activated the thrusters. They were still warm and running smoothly, so he looked at all the sensors as he had seen his owner do. That was also a part of human illogic, since they weren't mobile, they were always all there.

Outside, the Halmarins were pulling their weapons, getting ready to fire at the ship. Cge knew their hand blasters were ineffective against the metal hull, but ConekHayden would have said it was time to hop it.

He was still leaning sideways, peering out of the side of the view port, when he pulled back on the flight controls. The ship rose, yawing to port, causing the short Halmarins to drop to the ground.

Cge's computer wasn't stressed by scaring them, but he didn't think he should be going sideways, so he pulled the control back to compensate. He yawed in the other direction.

Too much compensation. He tried again in the other direction. He whistled as he slid so close to a stone building that he could have counted the stones in the top of the wall.

He decided he didn't quite have the touch, but he was rising, and moving up into the upper atmosphere. Below him Halmarin-IV appeared to be swinging back and forth. Two small inner-atmospheric hoppers had taken off in pursuit, but they were dodging about, dipping and soaring every time he changed direction.

If he was able to straighten the ship out, they would start firing at him, he decided, so he risked taking one hand from the controls to activate the planetary coordinates data file and saw the last listing, the one for Secundus.

Whistling his relief he punched his choice and activated the time-comp. He must have straightened the ship out, he decided, because a flash of blaster fire went by close overhead just as he saw the darkness of the Halmarin night gray as he went into time.

Jumps within a system were short and he didn't leave the cockpit. He spent his time trying to stop the unbidden questions from his computer about what he was to do if he had miscalculated and he came out during the Secundus day and glitched in the magnetic storms.

There was nothing he could do, he thought, but the distance was short by time-comp standards and when he came back into normal space he was on the dark side of the planet, shielded by it from the solar interference.

The ship's sensors picked up another vessel and identified it as *Traveler*. It had apparently picked him up too.

"Gella, I'll never forgive you for that—unless you found your ship." Androthemajor sounded angry.

Cge had been careful in his calculations and was sure he had done the correct thing, but the major's temper caused him to readjust his conclusions. Knowing Lovey-I was with Major Avvin, he whistled his news to the larger droid and instructed him to explain.

"*Cge?*" Androthemajor's voice rose a pitch as he overrode Lovey-I's slow explanation. Aboard *Windsong*, Cge could hear Deso speaking.

"That little *droid* is programmed to fly?" The human voice was Olvar. Cge wanted to ask why he was aboard the Skooler ship and Androthemajor on the Osalt freighter, but PilotOlvar sounded as if he were accusing ConekHayden of having done something he should not. To Cge it was more important to defend his owner.

"Cge does not have a program, but Gella has been taken by the Halmarins!" To him he had done what was logical in coming to get Androthemajor.

"Cge, you'll have to land the ship," the major said. "Olvar, you'll come back aboard here, and Drumps will have to take *Windsong*."

While Androthemajor made his plans, Cge started his descent. Below him Secundus was swinging back and forth as Halmarin-IV had done.

"No, Cge, don't try to land," Andro said hurriedly. "You'll never make it on this terrain."

"There is danger in allowing Cge to continue to pilot that vessel," Deso spoke up. "He is subject to random malfunctions."

Cge gave his assembly mate his opinion in a few well-chosen whistles.

"He needs smooth terrain," Androthemajor said. "The best place is back on Halmarin-IV. We just have time to get there if we leave now."

"I really must protest, Major," Drumps objected. "I should be at my experiments instead of in the cockpit, and I don't think the Halmarins would appreciate an unauthorized visit from us."

"I don't care what they think," Andro retorted. "You heard Cge! They made her a promise and didn't keep it. If they get blown all to hell I could care less, but we'll get her out if we have to attack the capital!"

"Really. I can't be a part—"

"You'll do it, or I'll blow the hell out of you," Olvar snarled. "Icor was a friend of mine."

"Olvar, love, you are becoming absolutely loquacious," Andro said. "I am in complete sympathy, though I cannot understand why that old smuggler had so many friends. Now, Cge, sweetie, punch up the coordinates listed as 'back-check' and read them out."

Cge did as he was told and on Androthemajor's order, he started his ascent out of the atmosphere, preparing to comp.

A check of his screens showed two blips for ships. He looked again. Yes, there were two, but the old CC-12's sensors should not be able to pick up the Skooler ship.

Perhaps it could. He had no computer time to give the second blip.

Just as he was punching the time-comp, a streak of blaster fire passed under him. Then he saw a second.

Was someone shooting at him? Before he could finish his question he was back in the gray of time-comp again.

No one could have been firing at him, he decided. The Halmarins had, but they had not had a ship in the air to follow him.

Was he recalling shots on Halmarin that his computer had not acknowledged then, but were in his data banks?

That's what it was, he decided, and hoped it didn't happen again. This was no time to glitch.

CHAPTER 27

Cge had been correct. The CC-12 had not been able to pick up *Windsong*. The second ship, flying too low to be read on the sensors aboard the Skooler ship or *Traveler*, had been a modified CU-35, a sleek military command vessel that had been camouflaged to hide its identity. Onetelles had been flying it when he had escaped the final Amal defeat.

He had been searching for some of his ships that had been warned off in time to escape the VladPat net on Vilarona. He'd eaten that fool Chukin who had used the one registration number that could cause him so much trouble and allowed that lo-head to be captured.

He'd found some of his people and sent them to search for the CD-51 the Halmarins had impounded. He had wanted the shipment, but they hadn't found it, and there was no point in continuing the hunt. Too much time had elapsed. The shipment would be too unstable to risk using.

The people he controlled by iocineil would just suffer. A few of them would die, but that would give the others plenty to think about.

He had suffered a setback in his plans, but if he could get the remnants of his organization together again, he would soon be back in the business of preparing to bring his people off Kayarsit-III.

He had heard Major Avvin was flying around the sector in an old CC-12, but he couldn't believe his good fortune when he saw the ship come out of time. His sensors had identified it, but there were a lot of old CC-12s around.

Then he'd heard Avvin's voice and abandoned his search. This time he would get him. That old CC-12 was no match for his ship.

He raised his ship and then poured on the speed when he heard Avvin requesting coordinates for Halmarin.

He was able to get off two shots at the old freighter before it grayed into time-comp, but he'd missed.

He still wouldn't lose his chance. With his perfect recall, he'd just fed the figures into his own computer and followed.

Avvin wasn't getting away again.

CHAPTER 28

"Damned dark place," Lesson griped as he checked the temperature on Anubis's outer hull. Ice was obscuring his view ports.

Rilvik, called the third habitable planet in the Halmarin system, contended with Secundus for second place in the line of planets. They shared an orbit, chasing each other around their sun.

Rilvik circled its sun once every four standard months. Its own rotation gave it a day's length of more than four hundred standard years. One side of the planet was an inferno, while the other was perpetually a dark frozen wasteland, twisted and tortured from its time in the sun. Around the terminator line the temperatures were habitable, but the atmosphere was toxic.

When Quinta Norden had boarded Conek's ship she had brought file data about the Halmarin system and the surrounding area. One of the facts that had marginally interested Lesson was learning that Rilvik was slowly overtaking Secundus. A million years or so in the future, the two would collide.

No loss, he thought.

He and Ister were searching the dark side of the terminator

line. Centuries before, the cooling of the heat-volatile surface had solidified it into crags, peaks, and gorges that could obscure any number of ships. It was a perfect place to hide the smuggling ships that had been using Vilarona as a base.

Too far from the terminator line on the dark side, the temperatures were too cold for the ships to maintain life support for long without running their thrusters. Much farther into the light and the magnetic storm would glitch the computers and the search would be futile. Not that he expected them to leave anyone aboard *Starfire* if it were there, but they would want to be able to move the ship later. At least he had to suppose they would.

"I sure as hell hope it's here," Lesson grumbled. "I'd hate to think I wasted my time in a place like this."

"Rather be on Beldorph," Ister answered over the commlink. "At least we could see."

"*Rather* be in the Singing Star," Lesson retorted, speaking of his favorite bar on MD-439. Turning strictly legal hadn't suited him at all until he discovered Tsaral had no objection to old customers returning to the smugglers' town to spend their honest money.

"Anyplace rather than here," Ister agreed as they searched the dark surface of the planet for any sign of life or ships.

Because of the ice on his view ports, Lesson was relying on his sensor screens. A blip close on his left came up so quickly it caused him to flinch before he realized he was picking up the Lapper.

"Anyplace but *here*," he shouted. "*I'm* here!"

"Then move over," Ister griped. "I'm getting storm interference."

Lesson spotted blips on his thruster sensors. Four. They were intermittent; at first he thought he was getting a glitch, but the terrain ahead was rough, and they were low. If they were trying to keep from being noticed—setting up an ambush—

"We're getting more than that," he said, clearing his blasters.

"Doesss *everyone* in FffarArm want to fffight?" Ister hissed.

Over the comm-link he heard the whine of the Lapper's weapons banks as they cleared and recharged.

"I'm getting tired of it too," Lesson agreed with the catman's sentiments. "Makes one feel downright unwelcome."

Then maybe the ships ahead—by now he could tell they were ships—weren't after him and Ister. Still it was better to be ready. This wasn't an area where trust was a homegrown commodity.

When the first streaks of fire went just over the top of the Osalt freighter, he knew he wasn't stepping too close to someone else's battle as they had done on Laver.

"Well, I been waiting," he muttered and fired off a shot at the oncoming ship. He tried to classify it but his computer's ident-data was going crazy trying to fit Hiddoran thrusters and CC fuselage with a computer conglomerate that made a Heinz-57 sound blue-blooded.

Whatever it was, it had some long-range boosters on its weapons that just didn't quit.

"*Down*right unfriendly," Lesson griped as he tried again, but he was too far out of range, though he had thought his boosters were the best made. His only chance to get off a telling shot was to get close enough, and to do that he needed to get down in the valleys and gorges where the boosters didn't help.

His only trouble was, with iced view ports he wouldn't have much vision and he never knew when he might angle over into the storm area where he wouldn't have sensor eyes either.

Still, he didn't have a lot of choice. To his left, Ister had put on speed, made a sharp descent, and the Lapper went off the Osalt freighter's screen. Lesson angled down, taking a shallower descent than the Lapper. His lumbering Warehouse couldn't turn or rise as suddenly as Ister's sleek little ship.

"You just weren't made for battle, old girl," he said to his vessel as he looked through the view ports and at the wildly gyrating ground elevation sensors. "It just makes me wonder how we end up in so many shoot-outs."

He shot down a wide curving valley and over a gap. Ahead he saw a low-flying ship, probably a Eacher system freighter, he thought. They were small and fast, nearly as quick as the Lapper. A good match for Ister, he thought, but the Orelian didn't seem to be around.

He let go with both forward blasters though he didn't expect any result, since he'd come up on the smaller freighter too fast to get an accurate fix. Then he gave out a whoop.

"We punched a good hole in his wing," he told *Anubis* as he dropped down into the next valley. He hadn't killed the ship, but it was too badly damaged for the tight flying in a fight and would be out of the action. That left three. He hadn't been able to get readings on the others.

"Ister. Make any of them?" Hell, there was no point in being quiet, since their presence wasn't exactly a secret any longer.

The cat-man answered with a spitting snarl, and off to his right, Lesson saw a stream of fire burning through the toxic atmosphere. Apparently Ister was busy.

Lesson now knew where the battle was going on.

"Let's go see if we can get in the game," he told the ship, turning hard to starboard. He didn't like flying around in gullies anyway, especially when there was so much metal ore in the ground he was picking up blips from pure deposits.

He had just finished his turn when he saw the sky light up with an explosion.

"Ister?" he shouted.

He was answered by another spitting snarl that told him the fireball in the sky had not been the Lapper. Watching his sensor screen, he saw one ship turn and head deep into the dark sector, and by the double wiggle of the Lapper's sturdy wings, Ister was after it.

"Thanks for leaving me one," Lesson muttered and took off after the second of the remaining ships. He set off a shot, swore at the near miss, and dipped to the left in *Anubis*'s slow-motion sideslip in an attempt to dodge the return fire of the ship ahead. The shot didn't make the distance; no fancy boosters on it.

It dipped and headed back into the canyons close to the

surface, but not before Lesson was able to get a reading on it. A CD. A fifty-one at that.

"Damn," he growled, watching it head down into a deep, narrow valley. What if it was *Starfire*? Conek and Norden were sure Gella's ship was hidden on one of the Halmarin system planets, and if old Charno-vins hadn't left someone to guard it, any smuggler could have picked it up.

He raised *Anubis* and followed the smaller ship from a higher elevation, trying to make up his mind whether to risk a shot.

"Got off one ssshot and he ssskipped into time," Ister said over the comm-unit, and Lesson saw the Lapper appear on his screen. "Let'ss get thiss one and finish with thiss planet." The Orelian was showing stress is his sibilants.

"Take a reading on the last one," Lesson suggested. "I want a closer look at him."

Lesson angled to the right, allowing Ister to flank the other side of the winding valley where the CD was racing along trying to lose the following ships. Since they could make speeds that would have been suicide for him, they kept a menacing pace.

Up ahead, the valley narrowed and came to an abrupt end at a shear cliff wall.

"You've run out of space," Lesson called over the speaker. "Rise out of that valley and you're dead."

"And if I don't I'm dead," a tenor voice answered. The pilot sounded resigned.

"Put it down and take your chances," Lesson answered. He wasn't sure what he meant by the remark, but before he could work it out the CD slowed, dropped down, and settled on the rough ground.

"Keep a lookout," Lesson told Ister and dropped to land by the small freighter. He was in his atmospheric suit in minutes and out of his ship, striding toward the CD. He didn't have to get too close to see the registration markings.

"Sleepy!" he shouted into the comm-unit built into his suit. "Tell Ister we've found *Starfire*!"

Wonderful, that was just what he needed, to find the ship

on a planet with a toxic atmosphere. If some chemical in the air set off the berecine before he could add the neutralizer—if they had shipped a neutralizer—hell, he wouldn't be around to complain about it.

He just wished he had had a chance to stop off at the Singing Star one more time.

The ship's ramp came down and the man inside was shaking with fear. By the rough coverall he wore, he was from the Eacher system. Then Lesson saw the sunken eyes surrounded by what looked like purple bruises and the convulsive swallowing that showed he was an io-head.

"They just told me to bring the ship here," the man said. "I don't know why they were shooting at you."

"So you just shot because they did," Lesson answered, keeping his hand weapon on the wretched-looking character, though he didn't expect any trouble from him.

"They ordered me to clear the ship's weapons. Firing was a mistake. I just hit the wrong button."

"Do just as I say, and you might get out of this alive. Now I need to get to the cargo—"

That seemed to confuse the io-head.

"Cargo? I don't think there is any—maybe in the back hold, but I didn't think there was anything on board." He stepped back hastily to allow Lesson to enter.

The old pilot had only taken two steps inside the ship before he stopped, staring at the passage.

The ship was a CD-51, the registration was Icor's, but this ship wasn't *Starfire*.

CHAPTER 29

"There's the gap in the mountains, just like Andro said," Norden told Conek.

"I'm feeling like he did," he muttered. "It seems a bit too easy. When everything goes too well at first something always goes wrong at the end."

"No negative thinking," the quinta ordered. "The planet hasn't blown up, so the berecine must still be stable for the moment."

"Tell it to hang on, we're coming," he said. "You're supposed to be going through that info."

"I am. The procedure is to ship carsmal weighted water with it."

"Sure, there's going to be a container labeled carsmal weighted water." Conek brought the nose of the ship up to clear the pass and dipped down again. At night, with the planet shielding them from the magnetic storm, the Halmarins could pick them up. He was keeping the ship as close to the mountains as he dared.

"They'd risk a giveaway like that?"

"Of course they wouldn't. We'll just have to open the containers. Carsmal has a distinctive smell, something like —blue ball flowers on Eminine."

"So what are they? What are they like?"

"Well, I don't know exactly," Norden hedged.

"Do you have even an idea?"

Norden sighed. "No."

"So how are we going to know the difference between berecine and this neutralizer?" He waited, but Norden didn't answer. She raised a pair of dark worried eyes before she shifted in her seat and stared resolutely through the view ports.

"By now there will be a vapor rising off the berecine," she said crisply. "We'll know what that is."

"And we don't even know they *shipped* carsmal stuff," he muttered.

But it was too late to worry about it. They were in sight of the abandoned spaceport. Conek flipped on the emergency receiver, but he heard nothing. Apparently Gella had not flipped the switch on her sender since she wasn't planning to leave the ship.

He had better luck with the ship's sensors. They indicated four metallic masses in the configuration of *Starfire*'s thrusters in one of the abandoned hangars. They also picked up the monitoring of a flight computer.

"It's here," Norden said as she watched the screens on the copilot's console.

"We're to be congratulated," Conek muttered as he set the ship down. "You'd better keep a lookout. We could be invaded by the Halmarins at any time."

"Then we'd better get aboard that ship," Norden said, unfastening her safety harness. "Do we wear masks?"

"Not necessary for a few hours," Conek said. He wasn't even sure of that. Hearsay was all he could get about the dangers of the clin-gas. He just couldn't be bothered. "People who are out to save the world don't wear masks," he told Norden as he led the way to the forward hold and released Lovey-II from his confining straps.

"You come along," Conek ordered the droid. "I may need help opening those hangar doors."

They had ridden the grav-rev beam down to the cracked plasticrete surface and were hurrying toward the hangar when Norden trotted forward to catch up with Conek.

"You didn't read all of Lesson's books," she retorted. "Or you'd know one hero in ancient times wore a mask and shot bullets made of silver."

She sounded breathless, as if she were chattering to keep from thinking about what they were trying to do. He didn't blame her. He didn't feel too good himself. He gave her all the encouragement he could muster.

"Why?"

"I once read they had creatures called vampires that could only be killed with wooden sticks and bullets made of silver. Maybe he was a vampire hunt—good galaxy!"

Conek looked up to see a ship shuddering with the strain of coming out of time-comp in the upper atmosphere. Whoever it was seemed to be in a hurry to arrive, he thought, then remembered no one could depend on anything with the computer glitches they were experiencing in that part of the Alpha FarArm.

They he recognized the CC-12.

"Andro should have better sense," he groused, not as irritated with the major for close timing as for finding out where *Starfire* had been hidden. He didn't like having his thunder stolen.

That reminded him that thunder wouldn't be heard over the roar if they didn't get those doors open and see what they could do with their canned bombs.

Lovey-II was more used to the light work of cleaning the staterooms than heavy lifting, but he heaved at the hangar doors with the strength of his programming, and nearly threw his owner off balance when they released and slid back. Conek was just glad droid muscles didn't atrophy.

He could barely see the ship, but he could tell it was a CD-51. His illuminator cast enough light for him to catch a glimpse of a ripple in the bulge of the first port thruster where a glancing shot had split the casing. The fused mend had been a sketchy job and imperfect.

That was enough to tell him he was looking at *Starfire*. He had done the fusing, and Gella never let him forget his sloppy work.

He'd remembered to bring the emergency entrance key,

and he inserted it in the belly of the ship, hoping Gella hadn't stored anything on top of it. Fortunately she hadn't. He was just climbing into the rear hold of the CD when Norden came racing up, her eyes wild.

"Someone's shooting at Andro!" she said. "We have to do something."

Conek stopped and looked back at her.

"What do you suggest?"

Norden's face paled. She looked as if she had been kicked in the stomach. Conek wished someone had been around to kick him. Andro was her only living relative, but after her first shock, she was too conscious of the public welfare to turn her back on the berecine in order to rescue her nephew.

"He can handle anything up there," Conek assured her, knowing he'd be biting his tongue off if anything happened to the major.

"Let's get this thing done," Norden said, climbing into the ship behind him. She didn't have to say that if they were quick enough they might be able to get back aboard *Bucephalus* and go to his aid.

Conek flashed his illuminator around the hold. It was empty. Reasonable. The rear hold would have been loaded with the first shipment to be delivered. The cargo for Vilarona would have been Gella's last stop so it should be the farthest forward.

Norden had hurried forward, but Conek stopped in the second hold to check. Gella could have had another route planned, but nothing in the second hold was marked precidine.

"Any luck?" he shouted at Norden through the hatch.

"I'm checking! Will you tell Lovey-II to stop that whistling? I can't hear myself think!"

Conek realized it was bothering him too.

"Two, will you stop that caterwauling—" But as he turned to finish his order he realized the big droid was standing right behind him, and wasn't making a sound. Lovey-II's attention was on the whistling coming out of the comm-link speakers wired into all the holds.

"What's going on?" he demanded. He'd had the Skooler

droids long enough to recognize urgency in their language even if he couldn't understand it.

"I have no memory of Cge being programmed as a pilot." Lovey-II sounded aggrieved as if it were his right to know.

"He isn't, what are you talking about?"

"Then how can he fly Androthemajor's vessel? Why is a pilot in an unidentified ship shooting at him?"

"*Cge*'s flying that CC-12?" Conek couldn't believe it but didn't doubt his little robot could get himself in just that sort of predicament.

"Affirmative."

Conek had started for the emergency hatch when Norden stepped through the entrance to the forward hold.

"I've found it," she said softly. "It's leaking."

"That's not Andro they're shooting at," Conek snarled. "That's Cge up there!"

"It's leaking." Norden's eyes were wide and dark. "It's expanding. We don't have much time."

She heard him say Cge was up there in that ship! He wanted to swear at her; he wanted to hit her; then he remembered she had been willing to turn her back on Andro for the sake of preventing the explosion. He could be expected to do the same for a mechanical.

It was just a machine.

It never worked right.

She had the right idea, get on with the job.

He thought she must have been made of stronger stuff than he was.

"That's Cge up there," he said again. "You don't understand, he can't shoot back."

"I understand there's a planet, a world of people in jeopardy, and we're here," Norden said.

Conek knew she was right. It didn't help. He followed her back into the forward hold.

"This is the last time I play the good guy," he snarled at her. "From now on it's strictly for myself, you understand that, Quinta?"

"Careful, Captain, move softly," she said. "Look at the bulge in that container."

Conek looked and felt his little critter sprinting up his backbone. She was right, the hard white drum had bulged in the middle. A tiny hairline crack was showing a trace of moisture.

What had the computer data said about berecine? As it grew more and more unstable it would first show a vapor as it gave off gases, and if enclosed in a tight canister when it went completely unstable—that part he didn't want to think about.

From the open hatch that led into the cockpit, he could hear Cge's frantic whistles.

"Hang in there, little buddy." Then Conek thought of the obvious. "Lovey-II," he shouted. He didn't worry about the silly name, he just wanted the droid's attention. "Tell Cge to comp out, back to Franklin—to Agnar-Alpha—anywhere, just get out of this area."

He started a frantic search among the white barrels labeled precidine for one without a bulge. If he could find one, and one only, that would be the quickest way to find the neutralizer, if it was there.

"Captain, don't shout. Don't set up any vibrations," Norden warned.

Lovey-II was whistling orders at Cge, but a voice cut across the message, a voice with the staccato clicks of an insect, yet it was not an arthropod speaking.

"Your shot was a little wild, Major. Let me show you how it's done."

"Cge is not the major," the little droid's musical voice answered.

"Pretending won't help you, Avvin. I should have had you on Delevort."

"Onetelles!" Norden and Conek spoke at the same time.

"Then turn around and come after me," Andro's voice also came through the open speaker in the cockpit and its mates in the holds. "You're wasting your time shooting at a droid."

"Droids don't fire ship's blasters," Onetelles answered.

Conek couldn't believe Cge had fired on the half-breed,

but something was keeping Onetelles convinced Andro was aboard the CC-12.

"Lovey-II, get up there and tell Cge that pushing the buttons on those weapons is not the same as playing shoot-out with Lesson!"

Lovey-II whistled, received an answer, and whistled again, this time imperiously.

"He does not listen," the big droid sounded aggrieved. "He will help to draw the fire of Onetelles."

"I'll tell him myself," Conek started for the cockpit, but Norden caught his arm as he attempted to pass her.

"You can't," she said urgently. "Onetelles wants me—and you—almost as much as Andro. If he learns we are down here and fires on your ship before we neutralize this berecine—"

She didn't have to say any more. Conek swore at the frustration of not being able to help his friends, but he turned back to searching the canisters.

"Here's one without a bulge," Norden said softly, as if she had not heard Andro issue an invitation that could mean his death. She worked at the top, trying to pry it loose, but without an opening tool, she wasn't having much success.

"Lovey-II, come help me," she said, raising her eyes to meet Conek's. "If this isn't it, we'll have to pry the lids off every one."

"We have to anyway," Conek answered automatically as he crossed the metal floor to join her. Their personal danger didn't seem as great when above them somewhere, Cge and Andro were vying to be the prime target for Onetelles's weapons.

CHAPTER 30

Conek gritted his teeth with the effort of trying to pry the top off the cannister without disturbing the contents inside. The one without the bulge had been the only one that seemed stable, and when they opened the lid they had discovered that blue ball flowers of Eminine smelled like dead chelovers.

They had pried the tops off two berecine vats, and half expecting to be blown into Holton Galaxy, they had slowly poured a liter of the carsmal weighted water into the first. It definitely made a difference. The berecine turned bright blue. It also stopped smoking and they were still alive to go on to the next one.

Conek swore as the bar slipped and banged against the wall.

Beside him, Lovey-II was prying a lid off with far more ease than Conek. He paused to give his owner a slow scan.

"Quinta Norden said you should not create any vibrations. The result of this stage of the berecine's instability—"

"I don't want to hear about it," Conek snapped, fitting the bar under the lid again.

"It is advisable to be informed of the dangers of—"

"Lovey-II, shut up," Norden ordered.

"I can shut *down*—"

"Don't do that," Conek said hurriedly. Trying to get the lids off the twenty-five vats without jarring them was slow work. Lovey-II, with his superior strength, was faster than Conek.

There were times when a guy didn't want to be bested. This wasn't one of them. From behind him came a little cracking sound. He and Norden exchanged glances and held their breaths. When nothing exploded he turned to look. Another leak. So what else was new?

He wasn't long in finding out. He heard the sound of thrusters. They were getting louder. They were getting *much* louder. Much louder in a *hurry*!

A vessel passed right overhead, followed by a second. The entire mesa seemed to vibrate. Conek reached out to hold on to two of the canisters as if his grip would keep them from shaking. He would have felt foolish if Norden hadn't been doing the same.

They heard an explosion and the ship rocked. In the dying roar of the passing vessels, they could hear the creaking of the old abandoned hangar.

"What does Andro think he's doing?" Norden demanded as she started for the cockpit and the radio. They could hear the incoming communications, but they couldn't transmit from the holds.

"Wait a minute, Quinta. Remember what you said about Onetelles? He'd know you were here."

"Then have Lovey-II tell them to draw him away."

"No."

Lovey-II had laid down the bar to follow the quinta's instructions, but he stopped and stood looking from one to the other.

"We can't help them, so let's not load on more trouble. One of them's already seen *Bucephalus*. They know we're down here. Our best chance is to finish. How many to go?"

She didn't need to answer. A quick look around the hold showed they had opened and neutralized eight. They had seventeen to do.

They heard another small crack. Neither turned to look.

Conek struggled with the metal bar on a lid that seemed

to be welded shut. Norden stood ready with a liter of weighted water to pour.

Maybe it wasn't the lid, maybe it was him, he thought as his sweating hands lost their grip. He stopped, wiped his hands on his pants, his forehead on his sleeve, and took another grip.

Norden raised her head, listening.

"They're moving off. I can't hear the thrusters."

But they could still hear the transmissions over the comm-unit, Andro was ordering Cge to pull out, but Cge's normal computer glitch was working well.

"Cge malfunctions?"

When the little droid answered Andro, Conek paused, thinking of the magnetic storm and wondering if the little fellow would make it, but there was a smooth satisfaction in the droid's voice. Conek could almost see the three blinks that had accompanied the remark.

Just as Conek got the top off the ninth container, Cge gave a shrill whistle. The big droids' voices were too much alike for Conek to be able to identify the speakers, but he knew two units were answering that higher pitch that was definitely Cge. He was apparently arguing with the other units.

"What was that?" Conek demanded of Lovey-II.

"Cge says the ship flown by Onetelles is too fast for them. He has told Deso to put up the force screen and stop the fight."

"Why doesn't he?"

"Lovey-I says Deso has been ordered shut down by PilotOlvar. Only Deso can use the force screen."

"Olvar's with Drumps? Then who's flying *Traveler*?"

"MajorAvvin, since he is not programmed to fly *Windsong*," the droid answered.

"Where's Drumps?" Conek demanded. Was it too much to expect the scientist to take over the controls in an emergency? That's what he was paid to do.

Lovey-II kept opening another container while he whistled at full volume, which was considerable. Apparently he could be heard in the cockpit. A Skooler whistle reached them from the bulkhead speakers.

"PilotDrumps has returned to his laboratory. He is only programmed for flying the ship, not for fighting." The droid paused to listen to another whistled message. "Lovey-II says PilotOlvar is not well programmed for close flying either."

If he had had time, Conek would have sympathized with Olvar. Only his loyalty to *Bucephalus* kept him from publicly admitting the Skooler ship was the best in his fleet. She was sweet to handle in space, but her size made her slow and awkward within an atmosphere.

"Here they come again," Conek said, dropping the bar and grabbing at one of the containers that was precariously stacked on top of two others. While he had been getting a lid off one, Lovey-II had removed two, and Norden was rushing to neutralize them before the vibrations of the passing ships set them off.

By the explosions, a series of blasts had been fired at the landing field. *Starfire* rocked again. Something was clattering and falling inside the old hangar.

They heard Andro's voice over the comm-unit.

"Shooting at downed ships is your style, isn't it, Onetelles? Afraid to face one in the air? I think you're afraid to face me."

"Andro don't," Norden breathed as she hurried back to refill her liter jugs. They still had eight vats to open and neutralize. Two more had started cracking.

Conek grabbed Lovey-II's metal arm and pulled him over to the most dangerous ones.

"Find out, come back and face me," Onetelles returned the jibe.

"I'm right behind you!" Andro shouted so loud the speakers on the CD-51 distorted his words. "I'll prove it. Here's three shots. *Damn* it, Cge, *stop firing!*"

"Damned little idiot," Conek growled. He didn't have to be told Cge had fired the CC-12's weapons three times. "Lovey-II, pass the word, Olvar is to turn off his comm-unit and order Drumps to activate Deso so he can get that screen up."

"Affirmative."

Conek didn't dare stop working, but out of the corner of

his eye he saw Lovey-II methodically remove the top off another container while he relayed the order. He decided he really liked that droid.

"They're coming back again!" Norden said, hurrying over with more weighted water. "How many more?"

Conek looked around. "Three."

He went to work on one while Lovey-II moved on to the next. Norden was standing with a liter jug in each hand.

Above them the sound of thrusters was getting closer, louder, the vibration was worse than before. Lovey-II raised his head to listen for a moment before returning to work.

"Three incoming vessels are slowing. They are not ships known to me, and none is the ship that is fighting with MajorAvvin."

"Locals, and they'll be landing," Conek said grimly. He worked off the lid and stood back for Norden to do her stuff. His immediate job was done. Lovey-II had already started on the last one.

The roar of the incoming ships was setting up a vibration in the old hangar. Something heavy and, by the clang, metal fell against the ship, causing it to rock.

"Hurry with that lid," Conek said, dropping his bar and holding on to the sides of the barrel the droid was trying to open.

"It is recalcitrant," Lovey-II said, working slowly around the lip.

"Who taught you that word—don't answer, just keep working at it." Conek didn't dare rush the droid. One of the Halmarin ships—if that's who they were—seemed to be hanging right over them, and the vibration was shaking the ship until Lovey-II, with his faster-than-human reflexes and superior strength, was having trouble keeping the prying bar under the lid.

They didn't hear the footsteps, and from across the compartment they barely heard the voices of the Halmarins who rushed into the ship with their side arms drawn. Conek recognized the Minister of Justice, Charno-vins, who accompanied a colonel and four uniformed guards.

"Keep at it, Two," Conek ordered the droid. He kept his

hands on the container, hoping they wouldn't be overly anxious with their trigger fingers. Just keep things calm as possible until they got that last lid off, he thought.

As usual, Norden had other plans.

"Wonderful!" she shouted at the Halmarin Minister of Justice. "Did you bring the rest of your government? If this last container blows up, we wouldn't want to leave anyone of importance alive, would we?"

"Quinta Norden!" Charno-vins stared at her, the folds of skin around his face wobbling as he swallowed convulsively. "You mean that really *is*—"

"Berecine!" she shouted at him and pointed up in the air with one finger. "Now get that ship out of here before you set it off!"

Conek grudgingly gave the Halmarin credit for courage. Charno-vins nodded at the colonel who motioned for his men to lower their weapons. The Minister of Justice raised a hand communicator to his lips and spoke into it. When they realized their danger, every one of the wrinkled little runts had turned white with fear, but not one backed toward the door and the dubious safety of distance.

The vibration lessoned just as Lovey-II succeeded in removing the last lid. The Halmarin jabbered as they saw the vapor rising.

Norden poured in the neutralizer and they all watched as the vapors stopped and the solution turned bright blue. She sank to the floor, and at first Conek thought she had fainted. Relief had kept him in his kneeling position, and he turned to break her fall. She wasn't unconscious; her relief had caused her leg muscles to go flaccid.

"I didn't believe it," Charno-vins said, slowly making a circuit of the hold and the open containers.

Over the comm-unit they heard another whistle, Cge. He was putting all the volume he could muster into his distress.

"*Traveler* has been hit," Lovey-II passed along the news.

Norden made a small sound of pain.

Cge was whistling again.

"The vessel flown by Onetelles was also hit and has gone into time-comp," Lovey-II said.

"That damned monster comped out on me *again*!" Andro shouted.

At least that's what Conek thought he said. At the moment it didn't matter. Andro and Cge had lasted through the fight, and their immediate danger was over.

"I need some air, even if it's toxic," Conek said, slowly getting to his feet. He helped Norden to stand and they activated the hold ramp. They ignored the Halmarins as if the guards were no longer armed.

Since they had seen the berecine for themselves, neither the colonel nor Charno-vins made any move to stop them. Instead they followed Lovey-II who rolled down the ramp behind Conek and the quinta.

"I thought you told that ship to leave," Norden said when she heard the approach of another vessel, but when they looked up they saw three ships, one was an Osalt freighter, one a Lapper, and they were flanking a CD-51 that looked suspiciously familiar.

The CD was landing.

"But that's—" Charno-vins looked from the ship to the hangar and back. "It's a trick," he said.

"Yeah, but Gella Icor was the butt of the joke," Conek said. "Take a look at that stenciling." He pointed at the descending ship. "If that paint's not years old, it's the best job of artificial aging I've ever seen."

The Halmarin officer and Charno-vins exchanged gazes. Their folds of skin seemed to be shaking in unison.

"It must be checked," the Minister of Justice said and paused. "If you still have the protective masks, we will take them to the young woman. We have no wish to stain our souls by punishing the innocent."

"If you live to get them there," Norden cried out, pointing up, where the CC-12 was descending in an erratic tilt.

"Cge!" Conek took two running steps toward the CC, stopped and turned, heading for *Bucephalus*. Realizing he couldn't make the cockpit and the comm-unit in time, he demanded the hand unit Charno-vins was carrying. It was set on the wrong frequency.

While he adjusted it, the CC-12 yawed and jinked drunkenly, dropping fifty meters and rising a few just as suddenly. Conek wondered why the wings didn't break off under the stress.

"Cge!" he shouted into the hand unit, but got no response. He still didn't have it on the right frequency. He tried again.

"Cge, wait!" No answer.

He fumbled with the hand unit with shaking fingers, stepping back when Norden tried to take it from him.

The CC was dropping again, swaying back and forth as if it were swinging on a cable. Two hundred meters from the ground it plummeted down, came to a sudden stop two meters from the surface, tilted, and then hit the landing pad with a thunk.

Conek and Norden sprinted toward the ship. They had not quite reached it when the hatch opened, the ramp lowered, and Cge rolled out, his sensor panel blinking rapidly.

"Cge is a *good* pilot!"

CHAPTER 31

A standard month after Conek and Norden had neutralized the berecine, Conek was on his way back to Agnar-Alpha after making a lucrative freight run, feeling everything was right in his world again.

It had taken a week for the Halmarins to decide the ancestral guilt for the death of their miners was not Icor's, and since that pilot was also dead, they were looking for his descendants. Conek hoped they didn't find any.

On the trip back to his home port, he thought about stopping off on MD-439 but changed his mind. After leaving his bride on their wedding day, Skielth had been enraged not to be in on finding either ship. He'd stormed off to his bride, swearing he was taking her on a tour of all three galaxies. He wouldn't be in the Singing Star, and Lesson just might be, though he was supposed to be on a freight run. Conek thought it best not to catch him.

Sis-Silsis was off on Farrat, unloading fifty of his slithers who were old enough to be taught the cynbeth ways. The rest of Conek's pilots were trying to catch up on the hauling contracts—all except Gella who had been grounded to be sure she had no ill effects from the clin-gas.

Conek had to admit Norden and Andro had been right about

leaving Lagon Fellerd to the authorities. He had talked as if his life depended on it, and when they found out he had worked for Onetelles, they could understand why.

He had been the only one who knew the half-breed's plans. When Norden learned that Onetelles planned to bring many, if not all of his people off the planet, she had ordered a cordon around Norther, as it had been called in later years.

Yep, everything was back on schedule, and before long, Conek hoped to be able to take some time off, to go to one of those pleasure planets advertised on the little travel holos he still collected.

He came in over Agnar-Alpha and eased *Bucephalus* through the heavy traffic of Agnar-Alpha's port. He dropped down to land in front of the huge abandoned government hangars he leased to house his Osalt freighters.

Starfire was in the last of his hangars, her inspection plates open while she went through a complete servicing. He had overridden Gella and insisted on having it done by the spaceport technicians to clear the ship of suspicion.

Next to the five buildings he leased, the doors were open on a smaller structure. The military must be moving back into the area, he thought, seeing the number of Vladmn ground patrol vehicles parked near the entrance. A platoon of guards stood at the ready, their weapons brought into firing positions as he landed.

"Hello, honey, I'm home," he muttered. "What's for dinner besides blaster bolts?" He was going to yell at somebody about something. He didn't like the idea of some trigger-happy recruit shooting at him because he didn't know Conek had a right to land in that area.

"Fragile cargo," said Lovey-II, who had been standing behind the pilot's seat during landing.

"Are you glitching again?" Conek demanded.

"It is LieutenantMarwit." Cge pointed toward the entrance of the small hangar.

"What's the commander of the quinta's guard doing here?" Conek felt stupid, asking the droids who couldn't know either. He didn't feel any better when Lovey-I, strapped in behind the copilot's seat, explained that to him.

Just then a small, slight figure appeared at the entrance and waved enthusiastically.

"It is Gella," Cge said, busily unstrapping himself from the copilot's seat. In a flash he had crawled down and was zipping through the passage that led to the lounge, followed by the two larger units. Conek hadn't finished shutting down the thrusters when he heard the lounge elevator's motor activated.

"Hey, wait for me, you mechanical . . ." He'd come up with an insult later. It didn't matter. They didn't wait.

When he reached the paved landing surface, they were already entering the hangar. The guards were watching them uneasily, but no one tried to stop them. He followed more slowly.

Inside he saw the old CC-12 Andro had appropriated from the confiscation station on Chalson-Minor. Four old thruster pods were lying against the side wall. The rear of the ship was mostly four gaping holes. On the starboard, a gleaming new Defcon-88 thruster was suspended on a grav-lift, ready to slide into one of the vacancies.

"I think I've found one that will work, Quinta," Gella shouted from somewhere beyond the pile of discarded thrusters by the wall.

"Well, bring it here, love, before I fall and injure something unmentionable," Andro shouted back.

"What's going on?" Conek demanded with a stentorian shout.

"Hello, Captain Hayden." Quinta Norden stuck her head out of the upper starboard hole that would later hold the suspended thruster. He recognized her by her voice. If she hadn't spoken, he wouldn't have had a clue. A pseudo-skin cap was molded to her head, protecting her hair. Her face was black with grease. "How do you like our new hobby?"

"Your what?" There was something about this that Conek didn't like. He'd figure out what it was after he stopped yelling. It took a while. For the present he concentrated on the fact that quintas were supposed to be off somewhere unreachable, running the government and not filling his landing pad with armed guards and badly parked vehicles. Shouldn't those guards be out somewhere making the galaxies safe for freedom and the Vladmn way of life or something?

He thought up a few choice remarks about majors who were in charge of port authorities. Since their jobs involved finding infractions that kept busy pilots from going about their business, he decided those comments could wait.

"I work hard in my position, Captain," the quinta answered. "Every psychological study proves hobbies are good for relaxation, particularly for people in high-stress jobs. And just in case you haven't noticed the date, it is first fifth, and every government office on the planet is closed. I can do what I like with my holiday. We won't bother you; you won't even know we're here."

"And despite your objections, love, we bought the ship at auction, and we're restoring it," Andro announced from his position on top of the suspended thruster.

"I am programmed for ship maintenance and repair," Lovey-II announced and rolled forward.

"I have the same programming," Lovey-I said and followed his assembly mate.

Cge was rolling along behind.

"What do you think you're doing?" Conek demanded of his defecting mechanicals. "You'll get filthy, and if you think you're going to roll through the lounge covered with grease, you're suffering from major malfunctions! You'll ride the grav-lift back in the hold!"

"I am programmed to ride the grav-lift," Lovey-II said and started climbing up the rear of the ship.

"I will assist." Lovey-I added, rolling toward the ship. "I am programmed as the emergency pilot for MajorAvvin."

"I've got better things to do," Conek groused, trying to think up some emergency. He'd have to heat his own meal, since Lovey-I would be too greasy to do it for him.

He didn't want anything to do with that ship. It seemed to him that Andro and the quinta spent enough time meddling in his affairs. With their own private vessel, they'd be on his tail every time he left the planet.

Hell, he was honest, but there was still some lucrative work on the other side of the law if he looked around. He still hadn't forgotten that illegal market for hermil on Niltea.

He turned, stalking toward the big doors, thinking he just might take a ride over to Siddah-II and see if Lesson was over there.

"I will also help," Cge announced in his high, piping voice. "I am programmed to ride the grav-rev beam, and I am capable of flying this ship."

"No!" Gella raised up from where she had been kneeling in her search around the old thrusters.

"No!" Andro slid forward on the suspended thruster and fell off, stumbling as he landed and staggering to keep his balance.

The little droid retracted his wheels with a clang. Conek didn't have to see his sensor to know it was blinking rapidly.

"But *Cge* is a *good* pilot," Cge announced.

Norden stuck her head out of the rear of the ship.

"Captain, do something with him!"

Conek grinned and strolled out of the hangar without looking back. He was leaving three humans and two droids to deal with Cge. Five to one—Cge had them outnumbered.

They just didn't know it yet.

WELCOME TO A FANTASTIC WORLD OF DANGER AND INTRIGUE!

Simon Hawke takes you where you've never dreamed...into a fantasy universe of wizards, wonder and terrifying excitement.

- ☐ **THE WIZARD OF RUE MORGUE**
  0-445-20740-3/$4.50 ($5.95 in Canada)
- ☐ **THE WIZARD OF SUNSET STRIP**
  0-445-20702-7/$3.95 ($4.95 in Canada)
- ☐ **THE WIZARD OF WHITECHAPEL**
  0-445-20304-8/$4.50 ($5.50 in Canada)

Questar
SCIENCE FICTION

Questar is a registered trademark of Warner Books, Inc.

**Warner Books P.O. Box 690
New York, NY 10019**

Please send me the books I have checked. I enclose a check or money order (not cash), plus 95¢ per order and 95¢ per copy to cover postage and handling,* or bill my ☐ American Express ☐ VISA ☐ MasterCard. (Allow 4-6 weeks for delivery.)

___Please send me your free mail order catalog. (If ordering only the catalog, include a large self-addressed, stamped envelope.)

Card # _____

Signature _____ Exp. Date _____

Name _____

Address _____

City _____ State _____ Zip _____

*New York and California residents add applicable sales tax.